HE'S SO GOOD

ROBERT & CARTER

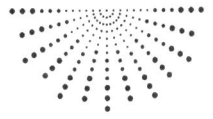

Z.L. ARKADIE

Z.L. ARKADIE BOOKS

ISBN: 978-1-942857-13-6

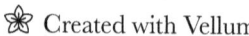 Created with Vellum

ACKNOWLEDGMENTS

Thanks to the following:

Edited by Red Adept Editing

Cover Design by Z.L. Arkadie

CHAPTER ONE

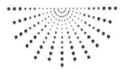

ROBERT TANGO

She moans, and it makes me harder. We're in the bedroom. I'm at Jack's house in Denver for Vince and Maggie's wedding. It's way past midnight. It sounds as if the reception party is finally winding down. I can hardly believe I'm doing this again. She's on top of my bed, positioned on her hands and knees, cheek kissing the pillow and ass up. I shift in and out of her steamy wetness, infatuated by her sexy profile. I'm giving it to her slowly, and it feels too damn good.

By the way she's moaning, it feels good to her too. But these deep, overwhelming sensations racing through me are not only confined to my groin— something's happening in my heart. The music in the distance isn't helping me contain my emotions.

The chords are slower than they've been all day—sultrier—and my thrusts are in rhythm.

"Oh, Robert," she sighs and bites the tip of her thumb.

"Shit," I whisper, trying not to let loose inside her. It's tough because I'm so fucking turned on. I'd been fighting the urge to make love to her since seeing her three days ago. We both traveled to Denver for the wedding. I was ecstatic when Vince asked me to be his best man. He said that I was his clear choice even though I'd betrayed him.

My excitement is about to explode. *Not yet.* I concentrate on not coming and pull out of her pulsating wetness. I push a deep breath past my clenched teeth as I grasp her by the hips and rotate her onto her back. I open her thighs and bask in the sight of her dripping slit. Our eyes connect. The seductive way she's looking at me makes me lose my head. My tongue itches to get a taste of her juices. She's been creaming since I plunged myself inside her. I close my eyes and suck in air sharply between my teeth. Suddenly a feeling washes over me, and my eyes pop open. My mind starts racing because I'm confused about everything that's going on between this sexy woman and me.

NINE HOURS EARLIER...

My phone buzzes in my jacket pocket. I forgot to turn it off. No one can hear but Vince and Maggie, who just recited their vows, but they're too caught up in each other's eyes to care. However, I did remember to silence the ringtone. I quickly reach into my pocket and smash the button to send the call to voice mail. Crisis averted.

"Maggie Conroy. Vincent Adams. I now pronounce you husband and wife. You may seal your vows with a kiss," the minister says.

With the kiss, it finally sinks in that Vince has done it. I was the only one who knew that he had an aversion to tying the knot. I'm positive that distaste had everything to do with his sisters pushing him to find a wife—one they approved of. They've been trying to indoctrinate him ever since high school. I spent many dinners with the Adams family, watching Maddie and Lexie deliberate about which of Vince's girlfriends he should marry. One criterion was that she fit in with them, and the more WASP, the better. Vince would never say anything as his sisters tried to run his life. His actions always spoke louder than his words. After we graduated from high school, his sisters tried to hound him into marrying Emily Callahan. He broke up with her two weeks before we left for college. True to form, I came in behind him and tried to fuck away her heartbreak. It didn't work. She tried to play the "I might be pregnant" card with him, which forced me to confess I'd been fucking her. I don't think she ever thought I'd tell Vince the truth.

As usual, Vince handled my slight against him with a halfhearted shrug and said, "I don't care," in a flat voice. I'm pretty sure he didn't give a damn. He probably was happy to be off the hook. Of course, after I confessed, she admitted that her pregnancy was a false alarm. I've never been the kind of guy a woman wants to trap.

Despite narrowly escaping Emily, Vince found himself staring into the eyes of a number of desperate and crazy women just like her. Then Maggie came along.

Maggie Conroy…

I've never bought into the idea of a woman looking her best on her wedding day. There's nothing sexy about a woman in a white gown with a headpiece shoved in her hair. I've always thought a woman was her sexiest in a bikini or, better yet, naked. But the sight of Maggie challenges my belief. She looks exquisite even through her tears. The both of them haven't stopped crying since Maggie started walking down the gold-paved aisle.

The idea of installing a shimmering gold hard-surface runner came from Monroe, Maggie's best friend. For the most part, she and Daisy, Jack Lord's wife, replanned the entire wedding at the last minute. It took a lot of money and competence to pull it off. I think it went like this: Maggie and Vince wanted to get married in the Hamptons, but Anne, Vince's mother, objected and talked them into letting her plan the event along with his sisters, Lexie, Maddie, and Allie. After much arm-twisting, Maggie and Vince agreed. Vince's sisters have always been experts when it came to manipulating circumstances to get what they want. Maggie quickly found herself losing control of her wedding day. Then, to make shit worse, Vince disappeared with only a few clues about what could've possibly happened to him. Maggie called her cousin Jack Lord, who rode into town on his white horse. Not knowing whether Vince was dead or alive, Maggie took off with Jack to look for him. I agreed to stay behind to look after the beautiful Mrs. Daisy Lord, who was tasked with tying up the rest of the wedding details. The guests kept rolling into town. Soon Maggie's best friend, Monroe, showed up and made it difficult for Vince's clan to get their way. Then Carter showed up, which made it even harder for me to forget and resist her. Eventually Vince was found, and now here we are.

"I now pronounce you husband and wife. You may kiss your bride," the minister says.

Vince and Maggie haven't plugged the water-works, not even while kissing. The air erupts with handclaps, whistles, and cheers. Everybody's happy. And I didn't see this coming—I rub the corners of my eyes. Damn it. I paste on a smile to keep from expressing the emotion that's brewing deep inside me. I'm so happy I want to cry too.

The ceremony is finally over. I join the constant applause. Vince and his new bride hold hands and prance up the aisle, kissing and hugging as they go. The band strikes up a tune in the tent, which is about three hundred feet away. Now that the happy couple has reached the end of the aisle, it's my turn to go. I can hardly feel my feet under me as I lead the rest of the party into the tent. For some reason, this very moment feels like the official end of an era. I can't decide if that sucks or if it's welcome.

Maggie and Vince are cutting a rug on the

dance floor. I move out of the way so Monroe, who's the matron of honor, can take over and lead the parade to the stage. Jacques Blanchard and his band are playing. I knew he was scheduled to be here, but I didn't expect him to actually show up this early. He told Daisy that he'd bring some friends to perform with him. However, he chose to keep the talent a secret. All he said was that the show would be a blast. And so far, that's how it's starting. I squint to make sure what I'm seeing is real. Is that Grammy Award-winning songstress Lida Cole on the stage? She's a pop chick that shakes her ass, humps the air, and twirls her hair. The only reason I know anything about her is because Zoe sometimes plays pop music on her computer. The song Lida Cole is singing now cycles through the playlist at least once per hour. It has a catchy and popular hook about a guy who finally "booked this babe before he booked it." I've accidentally found myself patting my foot to the tune. Which reminds me—I have to talk to Zoe about wearing earphones. The guests are howling with excitement. Even Maddie and Lexie are bopping toward the stage.

I gaze at the entrance, waiting for Carter to show up. I'm sure she'll have the same reaction to our finished product as I'm having right now. Since we're both architects, our skills were utilized to erect this magnificent tent. We spent most of yesterday directing the guys who set up the tent. Since we had our work hats on, I couldn't address the kiss we shared in my car on Thursday. Since then, I've been fantasizing about her. I'm having another thought of throwing her on top of the table in front of me, thrusting myself deep inside her while sucking on her tits. My pants get tight. Damn, she has the hardest but softest nipples.

Regardless how distracting she was, together we worked out the glitches to make this happen. We had to find the perfect spot to set up the three-thousand-square-foot tent, erecting it in perfect proximity to the ceremony area and pond as well as the stuffed sheep, deer, and rabbits, which sit in a fantasyland meadow Daisy and Monroe fashioned. Carter spent a lot of time helping the crew install extra framing to support the weight of the chandeliers. I managed the flooring and sidewalls. Instead of tarps, we used glass doors. Then Hannah, another one of Maggie's friends, came with her crew to style the interior. We all agreed to work as fast as possible in order to make it to a sit-down dinner with the bride and groom later that night. So there was no time to take Carter by the hand and lead her to a secret place to fulfill my fantasies.

I'm impressed by how well Monroe, Daisy, and Anne directed all the parts. It looks as if they paid a professional wedding planner a lot of money to conceptualize a scheme and carry it out.

Finally, Carter walks in, and she does exactly what I expected—stops to admire the ambiance. She catches me grinning at her and returns the expression. I like her—damn I like her. Then fucking Thatcher Collins, one of Vince's friends, steps beside her and touches her back. I open and close my mouth while watching Thatcher put his lips close to her ear and says something. My ego is crushed when she cuts her eyes away from my face to nod. I feel abandoned by the one thing I sought —her attention. I didn't know they knew each other.

The music dies down. Carter and Thatcher walk to a table and sit beside each other.

"Thank you all for coming to celebrate this joyous union," a woman says.

I set my glare on the stage, where Kathy, one of Vince's cousins, is emceeing. She's standing behind the microphone, smiling as though she's the bride. I focus on listening to her and watching Carter.

"Please find your seats right away. There are one, two, three, four, five, six guides that will help you find them. Guides, raise your hands." She giggles.

I already know what the guides look like. They are wearing white pantsuits and gloves. It seems Carter and Thatcher have already found their table.

"Once you're seated, your waiter will take your order. Each of you has a menu. Dinner will be served in three courses. Also, please do not neglect the bar. There are plenty of them set up along the walls, so you won't have to wait forever to be served a cocktail." Kathy giggles. "I heard at a certain time the only liquor that will be served is bourbon and rum, so load up on your champagne and cocktails now!"

Everyone finds the humor in what she just said, and laughter fills the tent. I locate the nearest guide and ask her to help me find my seat. The smiley young woman takes my name, checks her list, and asks me to follow her. I end up four tables away from Carter and seated between Monroe and Hannah.

Hannah looks at me with a wide grin. "Lucky me," she says with her lips close to my ear.

I back away. I'm not a happy camper although I

see how I ended up at this table. All three of Maggie's good friends are seated here—Monroe, Hannah, and Cleo and her husband Perry—along with Vince's buddies Pete, Josh, and Daryl—who happen to be my friends too—and their dates. Right away, the waiter takes our table's dinner order.

Monroe points at me. "Want a drink? Need a drink?"

"Nah, I'm okay."

"What? Are you sober?"

I shrug. "I'm not in AA or anything. I just want to watch my intake."

She tilts her head and narrows one eye. "Is today the day you want to be watching your intake, Tango?"

I laugh. "Okay, get me a bourbon."

She winks. "Now you're talking. And you, Hannah?"

"Champagne."

Monroe takes everyone else's order while she's at it. Once she's done, she traipses off to the bar to get our drinks. I've noticed that Monroe and Hannah have a love-hate relationship. I haven't decided if there's more love than hate or vice versa.

I'm looking Hannah in the eyes as she tells me she's going to be in San Francisco on business.

"I don't know how long I'm staying, but we should get together while I'm there," she says while twirling a lock of her hair.

My eyes gravitate toward Carter, and we lock gazes but only briefly. I wonder how long she's been watching me.

"I also dabble in interior design, and I heard you're having a hard time getting that part of your business off the ground. I can help," Hannah continues.

I clear my throat as I'm forced to look away from Carter. Hannah finally said something worth talking about.

"Maybe you can sit down with Grace."

"Right, Grace Kennedy," she says in a tone that indicates some familiarity.

"Do you know her?"

She measures with her thumb and index finger. "Some."

"Have you ever worked as an interior designer?"

"For a lucky few. I'm good at *everything*." Her tone is sexually suggestive.

I search Hannah's expression. Yep—she's making

a serious play for me, and I'm flattered by it. I've never been pursued by a woman of her caliber. And she's the type of woman who doesn't hear "no" often, if ever. Hell, I could possibly be her first no, and I hate to say it because I like her but not in that way.

"Listen, Hannah, I'm not sure what you're looking for from me…" I have to look away from her bright eyes for a second to recover. "But I'm in no shape to have a relationship."

Her cool smile grows an inch bigger. "I understand, Tango." She tilts her head. "We can be friends, can't we?"

I search her expression for deception. I uncover a kernel of it, which is not enough to cause alarm. "Sure," I finally say.

Monroe returns with a waiter, who passes out our drinks. Before taking her seat, she thanks the young guy, who's actually the bartender, for being so nice.

He pastes on a flirtatious grin. "Any time."

Monroe rewards him with a wink and turns her attention back to those of us seated around the table. The conversation turns to how beautiful everything is, and I somehow find myself answering a barrage of questions from Cleo, Hannah, and

Monroe about leaving A&Rt Media and starting my own company in San Francisco.

"If you asked me a year ago if that would even be possible, I would've one-hundred percent, hands down, said no," Cleo says, slapping the table. "Because, Tango, excuse my English, but you were a loser."

She says that with a straight face. I hesitate as I nod. "I'm sure there was a compliment somewhere in there."

"It was a compliment," Cleo says more emphatically. "Look at you. I actually took the time out of a busy hour to read a whole article about you in…" She snaps her fingers as she tries to remember.

"*Money Masters,*" her husband, Perry, says. "*MM.*"

"So now instead of a scoundrel, you're a money master," Monroe says with a snicker.

"How would you like to be on my show?" Cleo says in a rush.

All eyes are on me as she waits for my response.

"What show is that?" I ask.

She explains how she recently became the executive producer of Nightly World Bulletin with Ryan Juarez. I'm intrigued, and we talk some more about what a segment featuring me as a guest would entail. We're in a deep conversation about my early days at RT Creative when the announcer asks the bridal party and groomsmen to meet in the makeshift meadow for photos. At least Carter has broken away from Thatcher. Now she's having a good time posing with Allie and Vince. Maggie and her girlfriends pose together, then all the brides-maids, all the groomsmen, and finally, the two groups together. Before I can reach Carter, Thatcher snatches her into his arms, and Hannah pulls me into hers.

"You're with me, Tango," she says.

The photographer tells us all to say "wedding" and hold the *e* until he says to stop. We go through a variation of shots, and I sneak a peek at Thatcher with his chin on Carter's cheek as though they're a couple. Hell, maybe they are together. I decide to tune them out. Carter's better off without me anyway, at least for now. More than that, I feel like I can securely know that I was truthful with Hannah when I said that I wasn't in the mating mindset at the moment.

The photographer takes more pictures with Vince, Charlie, and Jack and then with Maggie, Daisy, and Charlie's longtime girlfriend, Angelina. It occurs to me that Vince has officially joined the

Lord clan, and just for a second, I feel a pinch of loss.

"Oh, and Rob too," Vince says.

Shit, I'm so happy that I can't stop smiling. I'm more than running—I'm fucking bouncing across the grass and taking my place in line right next to Vince, my brother, my buddy.

The picture-taking session ends, and we return to the tent for the first dinner course. I'm called up to give the first speech. Monroe pats me on the shoulder. "This ought to be good."

I'm momentarily paralyzed by her sarcastic tone. Hell. I rise to my feet. Expectation congests the atmosphere. I'm so damn nervous and unprepared for this. Vince didn't tell me he was actually going to follow protocol and make me get up and say something.

I clear my throat and blink rapidly, trying to focus on Vince and Maggie's faces. Why is this so fucking hard for me? Then a snapshot of me looking up at Maggie, who's sucking air and moaning as I eat her out, comes to mind.

I blink hard and loosen my tie some more. "Um…"

Monroe pats my hip. "Go to the microphone,

and take your drink with you. You're going to need it." She chuckles.

My eyes gravitate toward the exit instead of the stage.

"Right." I start walking through the laughs and claps. Everyone's amused but me. Shit. Once again, I wonder why this is so hard. I dig deep into one of my sessions with my therapist, Dr. Mahoney, as I drag myself up the stairs to the stage. I look at Vince as I walk to the microphone, wondering if he's thinking this might not be a good idea. A few years ago, neither one of us would have thought letting me give a wedding speech was a good idea. Nope. Me talking about our relationship in a room full of people would have been a recipe for embarrassing the both of us. First of all, I'd probably have been six bourbons in by this point and craving another go at Maggie's clam. I snicker at the irony and quickly turn to look at Vince when he does the same thing.

He and I grin at each other. We could always do that—have a full conversation without uttering a word.

I raise my glass. "To Vince and Maggie." I'm taken aback by the loud projection of my voice. I sound like a man with nothing else to say but that.

My eyes dart across the tables. Carter watches me with a curious expression. She and everyone else probably think I'm drunk.

I clear my throat and roll my shoulders back to stand up straight. "I know you're all waiting for me to say something witty or clever or whatever…" I take a deep breath to keep from hyperventilating. "Sometimes guys get up at weddings and say the dumbest shit."

There's laughter, and I ride with it until it quiets again.

"Vince and I, you know, we used to consider ourselves the nonmarrying type." I wink at the one person in the audience who would know that to be true. "My ex-wife, Lena, could confirm that."

Lena raises her arm, showing the thumbs-up. Maggie laughs the loudest before everyone else joins in. I'm pretty sure Lena and Maggie spent many hours gossiping about how lecherous I was on any given day. Just about everyone here knows me, so they get my humor. I nod at the floor, letting them have their moment while I wait until the laughing dies down. Once it does, I collect my thoughts and proceed.

"But for Vince, there was…"

I narrow an eye squeamishly when the image of a particular woman comes to mind.

Vanessa C.

Vince and I call her Vanessa C because we can never remember her last name. The C stands for bat-shit Crazy. She used to call Vince at least twenty times in a twenty-four-hour period, seven days a week, for as long as Vince could stand being in the relationship. She was hot as hell, though—long legs, the right amount of ass and tits, black hair, and intoxicating green bedroom eyes. She was one of a handful of Vince's girlfriends I was smart enough to avoid like the black plague. He finally broke up with her after he woke up in the middle of the night to use the bathroom and found her sitting in a chair across from his bed, staring at him. He'd thought she was out of town on a business trip. When he asked her how she got into his flat, Vanessa said she used his keys, all four of them. He'd never given her even one key. Apparently, she'd taken the keys off the ring, one at a time, and had them copied until she had the whole set. He broke up with her that night, and she left, kicking and screaming and calling him a lowlife player.

I scrunch up my noise as if the memory of the

next woman smells putrid as hell. "And then there was…"

Nicole Pitt.

Three months into their relationship, she bought herself an engagement ring on his behalf and told Vince it was time for him to ask her to marry her, being that she had let him fuck her one hundred and sixty-nine times and eight different ways in exactly ninety-one days. Vince and I had a good laugh over that, but he had to break it off with her then and there. She actually threatened to sue him for making a false promise to marry her. Vince never received the court papers, probably because no lawyer would take the case.

"And another, another, and…"

I close my eyes and wiggle my head at the thought of all the bad relationships that have vexed my friend. The worst of them all was Gabrielle Oslo, the daughter of the major investor in our media company. She made Vince commit to her by threatening to have her father sell his interest to our main competitor. Then yesterday I learned that Gabrielle was the one behind his kidnapping. And she didn't do it alone—she was assisted by another one of Vince's crazy ex-girlfriends, Cindy O'lay.

Finally, the mental picture of the next woman

paints over the others and takes the frown off my face. I turn to smile at her.

"And then there was Maggie Conroy. Her effect was immediate. She changed everything for him. She was a formidable woman—beautiful, smart, and unique." Vince puts his arm around Maggie and pulls her in for a kiss. An act that would've made me jealous in the past now makes me joyous. He deserves this after all the shit I put him through and all the crazy women from his past.

I take notice of the faces that are watching me. Somehow I have captured their undivided attention. Then my gaze falls on Carter, and I'm thinking that I sort of know exactly what Vince is feeling today.

"You may not know this, but Vince has been in love twice in his life. However, both times it was with the same woman." I smile, and after I realize my expression is directed at the wrong woman, I flick my eyes off Carter's face and look at Maggie. "Remember back in high school?"

She rolls her eyes as if the memory is torture. "Sometimes."

I chuckle, knowing that she has no fond memories of that year she spent at our high school here in Denver. "He loved you then," I say, nodding assuredly as I lift my glass. "Raise your glasses, and let's toast to fate. What a fine matchmaker she is." I wink.

Vince raises his glass higher. "To fate!"

"To fate!" the rest of us respond.

CHAPTER TWO

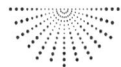

ROBERT TANGO

$\mathcal{M}$aggie's father, Isaac Conroy, gives the next speech. "You picked the right one, princess. And Vince, I know you'll take care of my diamond." He raises his glass. "To love."

We drink to love. Maggie's mother gives a speech, then Charlie and Jack, and then Maggie goes to the microphone. I've only seen her drunk twice before this evening. She smashes her hands on her waist and looks over at Jacques Blanchard, who's at the table with his band.

"Oh, Jacques," she sings. "We're ready to rumba!"

"Rumba time," the band sings in unison and flies out of the chairs like a swarm of excited bees. They take their positions onstage, and Charlie Lord goes with them. The chords of the song rip through the air, making a sudden impact. Angelina leads a line of dancers into the tent. I didn't even see her leave. They guide people out of their chairs and to the dance floor. The music is jumping. The excitement stirs my blood. The next thing I know, Hannah and Monroe are leading me down the aisle. I'm first inclined to look for Carter, but then I remember I'm letting whatever has ever gone on between us fizzle out. So I clamp my hands on Hannah's waist and let her dance us into the rumba line.

THE BOURBON, RUM, AND CHAMPAGNE ARE FLOWING. The dancing, eating, and laughing continue nonstop. One would think Jacques Blanchard and his high-profile band would've packed up and flown home by now, but that's not the case. So far, he's been joined by rocker Jeff Lowell, Steam Shirt, Debbie-G, Low Ground, Hiker, Devon Deville, Ace The House, and musical genius King. Then he plays and sings his own world-famous hits. Not a soul has left the celebration, not even the WASPs.

I'm at the bar.

"What would you like?" the bartender asks, batting her eyelashes.

"Tonic water with lime."

Her brows draw closer. "That's boring. Are you sure?"

"Oh, I'm sure." I'm already four bourbons in—all consumed at a snail's pace—and now's the time to cut myself off. One and a half more, and I'll be on my way to resuming bad habits, especially since Hannah has taken every opportunity to rub her tits and pussy against me while dancing. She wants me. Carter has been freezing me out from the get-go. I don't know what I did to deserve the cold shoulder, but hell if I'm going to pine over her. She danced with Thatcher and some other guys a few times, but mostly, she and Allie have stood near the stage, whooping, hollering, screaming, and shouting whenever a new act has come out. Like many other guests, I bet she had no idea Jacques Blanchard was going to actually show up and bring all his famous friends with him.

"Okay then, I'll have to go look for tonic," the bartender says.

"You don't have it?" I ask.

She winks flirtatiously. "There aren't many of you going dry tonight."

I'm stuck on how to respond when a hand slaps down on my shoulder.

I turn quickly, and my curiosity turns to elation. "Hey, buddy!"

It's Vince, and we hug.

"Had to find you to say thanks for being my best man."

"Thanks for asking, and brother, this is a grand party you have here."

"Yeah… it's perfect, especially after all the shit that happened."

Last night, Vince and I stayed up a few extra hours, talking about how wild it was that Gabrielle and Cindy kidnapped him just to keep him from marrying Maggie. He doesn't even want to think about what could've happened if they decided to take Maggie instead. That would've made for a far worse situation.

"Do you think they'll try something else?"

"Jack promised they wouldn't."

"How could Jack make that kind of promise?"

"He said he gave Pete Oslo a good talking-to."

The last time I checked, Gabrielle had her father wrapped around her finger. "Are you sure that's enough?"

Vince nods. "I'm positive."

It's strange, but he looks confident. I wouldn't be. The Oslos are bad news. Jack forced Oslo to sell him his majority interest in A&Rt Media and has managed to keep him off our asses since then. But I don't trust the situation. Over the years, I've learned to never turn my back on a woman scorned.

"She's good and crazy, but if you're confident in her backing off, then I'll join in."

He pats me on the shoulder. "Really. There's nothing to worry about."

Vince crosses his arms and starts rubbing his chin thoughtfully. "Anyway, so what's this I hear about you and Carter?"

I feel my eyes grow wide. "What do you mean?"

"Are you… you know?"

I shake my head spastically. "No…" I see myself making love to her next to my pool in Napa. "I mean, no."

Vince studies me with one eye narrowed, and I can tell he's not buying my bullshit.

"I have so much shit to work on. I haven't fantasized about fucking lately, let alone done it."

Vince shakes his head in sympathy. "So who called?"

I grimace, wondering what he's talking about.

"You got a call during the ceremony."

"Oh…" Now I remember. "I haven't checked yet."

I start twisting my watch around my wrist. I do this in therapy a lot, and Dr. Mahoney always asks me to take a deep breath and tell her what I'm thinking. The way Vince is looking at me, I can feel him criticizing me for not taking my business seriously enough to figure out who called. Hell, the sky could be falling at RT Creative, and I'm at a wedding, dancing, drinking, and—if I admit it— slightly disappointed that Carter is no longer interested in me.

"Here you go," the bartender says, handing me a glass of tonic water with lime.

Vince pats me on the shoulder again. "My wife is calling. Got to go."

"See you," I say, watching him walk backwards.

He points at me. "And hey, you've stopped drinking, but don't stop dancing!"

"I won't!" I take my drink.

The bartender says something about being the only one with tonic water on hand so if I want *some*, she's the only one who has what I need. Of course, her tone is suggestive, but I'm too distracted to be confused about how to respond. So I mumble thanks and race toward the exit. I sit on the edge of the fountain in the courtyard near the main house, take my phone out of my pocket, and turn it back on. The device chimes to life and shows me that I've missed nine calls and have two voice mails—all from Grace Kennedy.

My head droops. I wish I could ignore her, but the responsible thing would be to see what the hell she wants. I suck it up and call her back.

The phone rings once. "I'll meet you at the airport in DC tomorrow at three p.m. We have drinks with Elise Stein at six thirty and dinner at Tom Roth's house Monday at seven. Don't worry about suits or extra clothes. Mary let Zoe into your house, and she packed more of what you need. So that was the pretty important message that I left earlier, which you blew off until now."

Grace is pissed and wants me to feel the chill. I rub my left eye until my socket actually itches and my vision blurs. I sit straight, take a deep breath, and play along. "Who's Elise Stein?"

"She's the interior designer for the Atlantic Metropolitan Library Project."

"What do you mean?"

"I found out that we never had a chance of landing that project. Elise Stein Interiors has been hired since the beginning, and actually, so has your fuck buddy's firm."

I roll my eyes. She's talking about Carter. "That's enough," I scold. But what she just said hit me hard.

"So if I can't beat them, I'm joining them. However, I heard the deal they cut with Metropolis fell through."

"What deal?"

"That's why we're having dinner with Tom Roth. You're not going to ask who that is, are you?"

Grace is holding a winning deck right now, and she knows it. Sometimes it's hard to swallow the sugar and shit Grace dishes out. But she's said something worth hearing, so I answer her.

"No. I'm not going to ask you who that is."

"I didn't think so. Zoe's already emailed your boarding pass to you. Just in case you're fucking the enemy tonight, your flight leaves at seven. Don't miss it."

"Fucking the enemy?" I say, but she already hung up.

I feel my mouth tightening. If I could find value in firing Grace, I would. She's connected, and I want her connections. I look at the time on my phone. It's after eleven. Jacques Blanchard's band hasn't slowed down yet. The fact that there's no one loitering outside the tent says it all. All the excitement is inside. I consider going back in there for a few more turns on the dance floor, but since I'm not drinking and my flight is early, I decide to head up to my room and call it a night. No one's going to miss me anyway. Even Hannah finally backed off when Oscar Bettis started losing his shit over her. He asked her to dance four times before she said yes. Oscar went to high school with us. He's more Vince's friend than mine, but I owe him one for getting her off my ass. Two more bourbons, coupled with her continuing to rub her tits on me, would've made me regress despite my best intentions. And Carter hasn't looked my way all night. I let my eyes linger on the spotlight above the main entrance of the tent. Maybe I should go in there and ask her to dance. The thought of taking her in my arms and holding her close in front of Vince's family sounds like the stupidest thing I can do at the moment. I'm still trying to hide my feelings for her from them. They'd probably disown me as their adopted brother if they knew how much I want to dip my wick in her. But hell, I want more than that. I want to talk to her about architecture and shit. I'm pretty sure she's explored all of DC and discovered the most unique houses and neighborhoods. I want to know how often she goes exploring on her motor- cycle. But yep… first, I want to dip my wick in her. I drop my face and let my eyes adjust to the dusky pavement.

"Hey, Tango, what are you doing out here all alone in the dark?"

I look up. Hannah is strolling toward me, smoking a cigarette.

"Phone call," I barely say. The bad man on my left shoulder wants me to ask her up to my room so I can pound the hell out of her. I have some stored- up sexual frustration, and she's sexy as hell.

She sits beside me. Our thighs and shoulders are touching.

"So…" She blows smoke in the opposite direc- tion from me. "What do you want to do now?"

I cross my arms and lean away from her. This has got to be some sort of test. My mouth is half- open. All I have to do is say it. *Let's fuck.* But there's something holding me back. Every single time I've ever fucked a woman, it has all been about pleasing her. I want to hear each one moan and hiss for real. I don't stand for that faking-it shit. It takes a lot to get a woman off for real, but I've learned how to do it.

Dr. Mahoney helped me figure this out during our sessions. "What about you?" she asked.

She wanted to know if I knew how to have sex with the goal of only pleasing myself. When it came down to it, the answer was an earth-shattering, "No."

"Why not?"

"Because…" I shifted on the big, fluffy couch cushion. "That's selfish."

"Yes."

I shrugged to let her know that was the answer.

"There are a number of reasons and ways to have sex, and one of them is to satisfy yourself."

I'm still grappling with that revelation.

We talked some more about my issues with sex, and the more we delved into them, the more I thought I wanted to abstain until I got more clarity.

Hannah finishes blowing smoke in the opposite direction and then sets her alluring gaze on me.

Fuck. I don't want to please her, and that's why I don't want to do it.

"I'm…" I think better about telling her that I'm just going to go up to my room because I'm tired. I don't want her to get any ideas.

She raises her eyebrows leadingly. "I'm…"

"Hannah, get your ass in here. It's time to do the dance!" Monroe yells from across the grass.

I close my eyes briefly, relieved that Monroe saved my night. Hannah groans and smashes out her cigarette. "We're doing this surprise dance for Mags." She tilts her head toward the tent. "Come watch?"

"Maybe. I just need a second."

Her forehead wrinkles. "Are you okay, Tango?"

I wonder how she would know to ask that. I feel like I'm riding a rough wave on a surfboard. Maybe it shows on my face. I force a smile. "I'm fine."

"Leave Tango alone, and come on!" Monroe says, waving Hannah in her direction.

"Chill out. Jeez!" Hannah hops up and takes the cigarette butt with her. "To be continued." She winks and traipses off. I'm sure she's switching her hips for my benefit.

As soon as she's inside, my head feels as if I stepped off that surfboard, and my feet are on soggy but solid ground. I'm exhausted. I get up, and instead of going into the tent, I head to my room.

"ROBERT," A WOMAN SAYS.

My eyes pop open, and I sit up. She's kneeling at the side of my bed.

"Carter?"

"I wanted to dance with you, but you didn't come back," she whispers.

I blink a few times to make sure this isn't a dream. My mind is groggy. I didn't know I had fallen asleep. As soon as I got back to the room, I stripped down to my underwear and crawled into bed. The music is still going strong, and I remember thinking it was smart of me to hit the hay earlier rather than later because with all the noise, it was going to take me longer to drift off. Not only that, but women were on my mind—one woman more than others. It's been a while, and I'm horny as fuck.

"What time is it?" I ask.

"Who knows? But if you want me to leave…"

"No. Just, what are you doing here?"

Her broad and beautiful expression says it all. I scoot over and toss the sheet and quilt up, giving her the option of joining me. Carter rises smoothly to her feet. She takes a step back, lifts her dress by the hem, and pulls it off over her head. I've already grown wood.

CHAPTER THREE

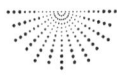

ROBERT TANGO

*C*arter shrieks and scrapes the backboard. Damn, I love feeling her pussy quiver against my lips. I made her come, again. I want to eat her pussy until the sun comes up.

She arches her back and then releases the tension in her body. "That was thirteen," she says breathlessly.

My finger prods her wetness as I watch her face. She looks just as intoxicated as I am. I've already come three times. We probably started going at it a few hours ago. The band has called it quits for the night. At some point, I got up and locked the door to my room, and good thing I did because Hannah came knocking, asking if I was awake. Carter and I stayed quiet until she went away. But the way

Carter's been moaning and whimpering, someone must've heard us in here by now. The good news is that Maggie and Vince are staying at the Ritz for the night, and then they're off on their honeymoon, which starts with a luxury safari in South Africa. Basically, Vince won't hear about how I fucked his cousin's brains out on the night of his wedding until after he returns—I hope.

"Damn it, you're so good at that." Carter cradles her hands under my armpits and pulls me up to kiss her. It's so hot when a woman delights in the taste of her own pussy on my lips and inside my mouth.

"I have to check something," I say after pulling my mouth away from hers. I reach over to the nightstand and pick up my phone. Carter curls up in a ball, hugging herself, as she faces the opposite direction.

It's 5:37 a.m. We've been at this for a while.

"Shit," I say.

She turns back around to face me. "What is it?"

"My flight leaves in less than an hour and a half."

"Your flight? Why are you leaving so early? It's Sunday."

I glance at her as I set my phone back on the

nightstand. We both know that her firm is in competition with my firm for the Atlantic Metropolitan Library Project, and she's just as hungry for the account as I am.

"Something's come up."

She sits up quickly. "You don't have a girlfriend, do you?"

I study her to make sure she's serious. She is. "No, I don't."

Now she examines me, probably trying to figure out if I'm being truthful. A guy with my reputation deserves that sort of scrutiny.

Carter flops back down on the bed. "Sorry. I don't mean to be so insecure. It's just that you're so…"

I lie back down beside her and wait for her to finish. She's gazing off thoughtfully.

"I'm so what?"

"Wanted." She sighs. "Wanted by so many women. I still don't know why you want me when you can have someone like Hannah Rossi on your nuts."

Thank goodness the blood is rushing back to my extremity because with that vulnerable look on her pretty face, I must have her one more time before I go.

"Listen…" I rub her rose-petal-soft cheek. I wonder why her mouth always begs me to kiss it. She has a slight overbite. I think it's one thing that makes her a fantastic kisser.

"What?" She looks as though she's trapped in my devouring gaze.

"I don't have a girlfriend. I don't want Hannah or any other woman—"

"I know," she says, cutting me off before I can finish. "And neither do I. No boyfriend. I'm too busy for one. We're just getting it out of our systems, Robert. That's all."

Wow. My boner deflates. I feel as though I've just run into a brick wall. I don't know what I want from Carter although I do know what I want for her. It's hard for me to picture another man sucking on her nipples and licking her clit, making her scream. I love it when she shivers. I've never been with a woman who shivers as intensely as she does. She fucking enjoys what I do to her, every second of it. However, the need to please women while not seeing that my needs are met is a problem. One night with Carter has just revealed that I still have the same fucking issues. But it felt so damn good. Different. I was present the whole time. That's different.

Exasperated, I sigh deeply and let it out slowly. "Yeah." I roll out of bed. There's a lot I want to say to Carter, but I have to get ready for my flight.

She scoots off the bed and picks up her dress. "Okay, then, I'm going to go."

"Wait." I gather her in my arms and look into her wide eyes. "Thanks for coming to see me. It was the highlight of my trip."

Carter lowers her head. "I wanted it too, so…"

I take her by the chin and lift her face. "How about I call you soon?"

She grunts, rolling her eyes.

"You don't believe me?"

"I mean why? You live in San Francisco, and I live in DC."

"That won't prevent me from calling you."

"I know but…" She shakes her head as if she wants to say something else but has thought better of it.

"But what?" I insist.

"Isn't Hannah going to work for you?"

I jerk my head back. "Where did you get that from?"

"Hannah said that she's going to be working with Grace for a while."

I frown harder. "Really? I never heard of it." I

41

quickly replay the conversation I had with Hannah at the table. She said she was coming to San Francisco for a while and I said that since she does interior design work, she should sit down with Grace. But truth be told, I wasn't being serious. Hannah couldn't have called Grace and weaseled herself into my circle that fast, could she? No way.

"Ugh." Carter groans, shaking her hands frantically. "What's wrong with me? I've never been this insecure in my life." She rips herself out of my arms. "It's because of you, Robert Tango."

"Me?"

"You. You're just too…" She rolls her hand around my form. "Too hot. Too rich. Too successful. And too damn good in bed."

"I…"

"You're like the fucking hunger games for women. Even the bartender was weighing her chances." She shakes her head and takes more steps backward. "I just can't… I can't do this right now."

I step toward her, and her hand flings up to halt me.

"Can I at least call you?"

She closes he eyes as if what I just said blew hot air into her eyes. "What for?"

"Because I want to."

Carter looks at the door and then quickly puts her dress on. She stuffs her bra under her arm.

"Have a good flight."

My lips part. What should I do? I want to catch her and tell her the truth before she walks out that door. I don't want Hannah or any other woman as much as I want her. And she's really wrong about me. I'm really too… broken. Too superficial. Too hurt. Too disgusted with myself. And too afraid to love her the way I want to.

And finally, too caught up in self-loathing to do anything about it, I let my shoulders droop, and she quietly slips out of my room and closes the door behind her.

THE HOUSE IS QUIET WHEN I TAKE THE STAIRS down. The sweet smell of fresh-baked something fills the hallways. I've already decided to call Jack later and tell him that I have to catch a flight and thank him for his hospitality. If only I could lodge at their house every time I came to Denver. Jack has me thinking and possibly picking up some tips on how to run a household. I still live in his Russian Hill home in San Francisco, and Mary, his in-home caretaker, is still cooking my breakfast and dinner mostly. When I'm home during the day, she makes me lunch and snacks in between. But the benefit of house staff is that I haven't had to go grocery shopping, and I haven't had to stop working on tasks to fix myself something insufficient to eat. I'm a bad cook. I hate to cook. Maybe because I had to do it for myself too much when I was a kid.

Before I can make it to the kitchen and ask for a taste of whatever's baking, I run into Jack and Daisy in the sitting room, which is past the living room. They're sitting across from each other, staring out the window at a small garden. They turn to see me at the same time.

"Leaving already?" the beautiful Mrs. Lord asks.

I set my bags down and walk over. "Yep. I have a flight to catch."

Jack stops massaging Daisy's feet. "I just wanted to say thanks for taking good care of my wife."

Daisy smiles. "I told him we were worried, but you and Monroe still managed to keep it light around here." Her sigh is shallow as if she's remembering some of those times.

"Well, you were the solid one," I say.

"She always is," Jack says.

I get to thank them for their hospitality in person. Daisy makes sure the cook gives me what she calls "morning glory beignets" and a to-go cup of spice coffee, which I consume while driving to the airport. It's all tasty and gourmet, the kind of food one expects from Jack and Daisy's kitchen.

As usual, Zoe has my schedule solidly planned. I return my rental car and take the shuttle to the terminal. Since I have carry-on luggage, I show my boarding pass on my cell phone at the security checkpoint, walk through the radiation zapper, and hike to my gate. There are times when I wish I splurged more on charter flights. My flight is already boarding, and I'm only halfway to the gate. I've become one of those nitwits who run through the terminal because they didn't leave early enough.

I make it to the gate, show the agent my boarding pass, and race down the jet bridge. After I give the stewardess my luggage and flop down in my seat, I close my eyes and grab onto a memory that can settle me. I'm tasting Carter's wetness. She's climaxing, and I'm loving the way her pussy throbs against my mouth. Damn, she comes hard.

"Can I get you anything to drink?" the stewardess asks.

My eyes pop open.

"I don't know about him, but you can get me champagne," Hannah says as she steps around the stewardess.

My mouth falls open. "What the hell are you doing here?"

She winks. "How do you think you landed drinks with Elise Stein tonight?"

I jerk my head back. "You?"

Hannah gives me an easy nod as she takes the seat near the window beside me. "So, um, who were you sleeping with last night, Tango?"

I'm still stuck in shock. Fucking Grace. She's got a lot of explaining to do.

CHAPTER FOUR

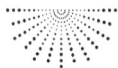

ROBERT TANGO

I must've been on a high after making love to Carter, but now I'm crashing.

"The door to your room was locked," Hannah says.

I nod slowly, struggling just to keep my eyes open. "I was in bed, Hannah."

"But were you sleeping by yourself?"

"Yes."

She laughs bitterly. "You're fucking lying to me. You don't have to lie. You're a big boy, and Carter's a big girl—in a way."

I feel my forehead crash down into a severe frown. I don't like the jab she took at Carter. My mouth has consumed just about every inch of

Carter's body, and I can assure Hannah that she's a "big girl."

Hannah draws back. "Oh. Did I offend you?"

The longer I blink at her, the more tired I become. "Yes. I was with Carter. Happy?"

"Hell no. But I'm happy that you finally spilled the truth."

I back up a little as I watch her face move in my direction. Her mouth stops next to my ear.

"I want you, Tango. Carter—I don't know what game she's playing, but I play no games." She finally gives me space, gets comfy in her seat, and closes her eyes.

I scratch my head. It takes a moment to realize something: I'm Hannah. She's pulling the same tricks on me that I pulled on Maggie and countless other unavailable women. I take a deep breath.

"Mr. Tango, you ordered the peppered potatoes and eggs Benedict?" the stewardess asks.

I rip my eyes off Hannah and clear my throat. "Yeah, um, sure." Zoe must've ordered it for me.

"And you, Miss Rossi?"

"Yes, same thing," Hannah replies with her eyes still closed.

"Excellent. Thanks." The stewardess moves on to the next set of seats.

I'm almost too exhausted to eat, but I'll sleep better on a full stomach. At times like this, I wish Zoe had booked the charter service. I'm always complaining about spending unnecessary funds on extravagance, but in this case, when I'm traveling as a worn-out businessman, I can use the service and isolation.

Hannah still hasn't opened her eyes. I know what she's doing. It's the most basic play in the wear-them-down handbook.

"So, Hannah, how long have you known Grace?" I ask.

She grins slyly. "A long time."

I grunt. "Why didn't you come right out and tell me?"

"What for?"

"What for? Look what you've done. You're part of my interior-design team, and it happened without my knowledge."

She puts a finger across her lips. "Shush. You're making me sound desperate."

"That was a pretty desperate thing you did."

Finally, she opens her eyes and looks at me. She's certainly a beautiful woman, but that's just not enough.

"Why are you even complaining?" She touches

her chest. "You have me, Hannah Rossi, with your team—not *on* your team, mind you. You would have to pay me for my services."

"What's the purpose of you being with my team?"

"I'm helping a friend." She says that so fast that it sounds like she's convinced herself of her own bullshit.

"And that friend is Grace?"

"Yes."

"And you're the one who arranged drinks with Elise Stein?"

"She and I go way back to elementary boarding school." She sniffs disdainfully. "Can you believe they allow parents to ship their kids off that young?"

I pause to examine her. I've never had so much clarity, and yet I'm still so confused. All I know for sure is that I can't see Hannah as a conniving woman. I refuse to judge her that harshly.

"Well, thanks for helping my team."

It takes her a moment, but she finally cracks a tiny smile. "You're welcome." She turns to look out the window. I know she's uncomfortable. That's exactly how I would be if I were her.

She faces me again. "Oh, and you may need me

more than you think."

I narrow my eyes. "What does that mean?"

"That means I love Maggie, and Maggie loves Vince, and Vince loves you, which means I'm going to always be on your side."

I'm pretty sure I get the gist of what she's saying. If it comes down to choosing between Grace and me, she'll choose me.

"Thank you," I say.

She shrugs. "Thank you for not telling me to take my sweet ass back to Denver."

I crack a tiny smile. "How can I do that when you're the one who landed us the meeting with Elise Stein?"

She winks. "True, but believe me, Grace has already figured out a way to hold all the cards."

I snort cynically. "Then you know her well?"

"Very well."

Hannah and I grin at each other as if we have an unspoken understanding. Breakfast is served, and as we eat, I keep Hannah talking about her ideas for the interior of the Atlantic Metropolitan Library Project. I'm impressed by how much she knows about our structural-design model. I get her to admit that she's been working with Grace's team for weeks.

"Grace and I ran into each other at the Met ball gala. I congratulated her on the sale of her father's company. I heard he got way beyond top dollar for it." Hannah winks at me in a way that says I was a fool for paying so much for a failing business.

"I'm making it back and more." I wink at her.

She snickers lightly. "Anyway, she went on this tangent about how much she despises you and respects you, both with equal fervor."

I grunt and adjust in my seat.

"I told her I knew you and that I almost slept with you."

"Yeah, you keep saying that, but I don't remember."

"And I keep telling you that you were high, which is why I turned you down."

I nod. "Right. You've said that." I've brought women to my bed only to fall asleep on them on numerous occasions. But in the morning, when I was half-sober, I made sure to reward them for sticking with me through the night.

Hannah snaps her fingers. "Earth to Tango."

I shake my head and bring myself back to the moment. "Sorry about that."

"Where did you go?"

"To an old place. Listen, I like everything you

said. Grace doesn't have the budget to add another team member to the project, but I would like to hire you if…."

"No." She shakes her head. "I don't want to work for you, Tango. I *want* you. That's the only reason why I'm here."

Once again, I'm speechless.

She chuckles. "Just kidding. I'm not that crazy." She pats my thigh. "Sure! I'll have my contract drawn up and sent to your legal department."

It takes a moment, but I end up laughing with her.

"I want to leave fashion styling for interior design. It's a better world as far as I'm concerned," Hannah says.

I ask her why, and she moves from one horror story to the next, starring starving models and frantic designers. Soon she yawns and tells me she has to catch at least three hours of sleep. I agree with her. I didn't expect to have such a good time talking to Hannah. I'm not surprised. She's Maggie's friend, and Maggie is just as interesting. The thing is, I'm still not attracted to her in a sexual way. I want Carter too badly—again.

So Hannah and I close our eyes to get some sleep.

CHAPTER FIVE

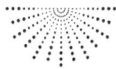

ROBERT TANGO

*H*annah and I are waiting for her luggage to exit the carousel at baggage claim. Grace is supposed to meet us here. She's not hard to spot when she arrives, wearing a neat red skirt suit with extra-high heels. Rain, snow, or shine, she's strutting around in shoes like that. A few women I've been with complained those sorts of shoes hurt like hell, but to see Grace in them, one would think they felt like two soft pillows. She's being followed by a guy in a black suit. He must be the driver.

The carousel starts. The first piece of luggage rolls out.

"There's my suitcase," Hannah says, pointing.

"Get that for her, Donald," Grace orders the

guy in black. She rubs her neck. "It's so humid in this fucking city."

I shake my head. I don't like her crass style. Yeah, she took the time to learn the guy's name, but she could at least say please.

Hannah holds up her hand. "I got it, Donald. Thanks."

Apparently, she and I are on the same page.

"No way am I going to let a lady as beautiful as you are pull that luggage off the belt," he says.

Hannah smiles weakly. I can tell she's torn. There's something else I just learned about her— she's an independent woman, used to doing it all by herself. It may have something to do with being shipped off to boarding school at an early age.

"Thanks," Hannah says as she steps out of the way so that Donald can retrieve her suitcase.

Grace grunts as if she's irritated that Hannah even offered to get her own luggage in the first place.

GRACE ORDERED A LIMOUSINE TO CHAUFFEUR US around. I'm sort of flabbergasted to see it. She knows a limo isn't my style. I choose a rental car according to how much fun I want to have, how many people are with me, and what sort of business trip I'm on, and I drive myself. And if I'm in a city like DC, I also incorporate some public transportation, especially if I have a meeting scheduled during rush hour.

"Why the showy car?" I ask as we get into the backseat.

"Because this is DC, and everyone's watching."

I frown. "What the hell does that mean?"

"Buckle up, Tango," Hannah says.

I'm still waiting for an answer from Grace as I latch my seat belt.

Grace raises her eyebrows. "You want to lock down this account?"

I can feel my frown grow more intense. "Is that a rhetorical question?"

She sighs. "Robert, you're cranky because you did exactly what I didn't want you to do."

Once again, I'm lost.

"Hannah already told me you had company last night."

I look at Hannah, and she shrugs. "She asked, so I told her."

I shake my head, muttering all the curse words I want to hurl at both women. "Let me be clear with both of you: my personal life is none of your business."

Grace raises a finger as she punches out a message on her phone with her other hand. "Sometimes yes, but not all the time, Robert." She says that so nonchalantly that for a second I question whether or not she's right.

"Yes, all the time," I say.

"Not when you show up for an important meeting in the shape that you're in. For goodness sake, I need you to make an impression. You do know that you have a reputation?"

I sniff bitterly. "You know you're a fucking dirty fighter, don't you?"

Finally, she looks up and sets her gaze on me. "Yes."

She and I glare at each other. *You're fired* is on the tip of my tongue, but I can't say it because I fucking need her. However, I refuse to look away first.

Hannah clears her throat. Neither Grace nor I retreat. Hannah clears her throat again. Still, our eyes are locked on each other like two pit bulls.

Then Hannah snaps her fingers in front of both of our faces. "Hey, hey, hey!"

Grace and I turn to look at her at the same time.

"Really, Tango, is this how your team operates?" Hannah asks.

"No, it is not," I say unenthusiastically.

I'm unsettled, but other than Grace monopolizing this whole process and me being exhausted from this weekend and last night, I can't find a reason for this icky feeling.

"I agree," Grace says passively.

I try not to glare at her. I have probably tolerated Grace for as long as I can stand. But I want the Atlantic Metropolitan Library Project. It will open the door to so many other opportunities, especially if we beat out Metropolis for the account and slay it with our work.

I set my eyes on Hannah. "All right. Tell me more about Elise Stein."

Grace starts to speak.

"She's connected," Hannah says.

"So her success is a result of who she knows."

Hannah winks. "But isn't that always the case?"

"So," Grace says louder than necessary. She's trying to win back the floor. "This meeting we have with her will be a precursor to dinner with Tom Roth."

"You have to convince her that she will benefit by working with *your* firm."

I jerk my head back. "But she's already working with *my* firm, isn't she?"

"KCID is *my* initiative."

I laugh with an edge. I'm about to remind Grace who owns KCID and who was smart enough to insert a clause in her contract stating that she can be released from her position before the end of the agreed-upon term as long as I have reasonable cause. The fact that she can't maintain employees for more than a hot minute, and is costing me an arm and a leg in unemployment payouts after she fires them, should be reason enough. However, I catch how Hannah is watching me with raised eyebrows. I suspect it's a warning look.

"Let's just move on," I say. "What do you think it takes to get Elise on my side?" My eyes shift between Grace and Hannah. I spend the next hour stuck in traffic, listening attentively as both women fill me in on Elise Stein.

We arrive at the Continental on the River Hotel, which sits along the muddy Potomac River. My room is on the top floor with big windows that face downtown. Hannah is in a room down the hallway, and Grace is across from Hannah. She asked Zoe to put her in the room next to mine since we would be working closely in the upcoming week, but once again, Zoe instinctively did what I would prefer and put some distance between Grace and me.

I fold my arms and grin as I look out over the DC cityscape. This is satisfying. The streets are just as energetic as Manhattan's, especially at this time of day. I miss the oomph. That's another reason I need to land this account—I'm ready to return to the East Coast.

Now that I've gotten an eyeful of the excitement, it's time to prepare for drinks. I shower and dress. Zoe had four suits delivered to my room overnight, and they now hang in the closet. She also chose shirts, shoes, socks, T-shirts, and ties. And she must really pay attention to what I wear because I would've packed at least two-thirds of these items. I wouldn't have brought the rest of it at all.

I've chosen to wear my navy Brioni suit. I take my gold cufflinks out of my pocket and put them on, along with a silk eggplant tie. If this isn't dressing to impress, I don't know what is.

I grab my wallet and briefcase and head out to meet the ladies in the lobby. I see them in the waiting area near the window. Hannah and Grace haven't caught sight of me yet, which gives me a moment to observe them. They're sitting across from each other, both engrossed in their cell phones. The more I watch, the clearer I can see that they aren't such great friends. I recall what Hannah said in the limo about Elise Stein—"She's a *who you know* person and not a *what you know* person." Grace is the same way. Was Hannah trying to give me a hint?

I keep my assessment at the forefront of my mind as I reveal myself to the ladies. They both hop to their feet as soon as they notice me.

"Ready?" I say.

"Let's go." Grace heads to the door.

"You look good, Tango," Hannah says with a smile.

"Thanks." I watch Grace. She's already getting into the backseat of the limousine. "What's wrong with her?"

Hannah shrugs. "I think she's still upset about not having a room next to yours. Maybe she wants to creep into your room at night."

I grunt at how ridiculous that sounds. "Who, Grace? No way."

Hannah nods thoughtfully. "I guess you're right.

She doesn't like you, and from what I can tell, the feeling's mutual."

I shrug at the obvious and walk toward the exit.

Hannah catches my arm. "Tango?"

I turn to face her.

"Grace wants something from you, and she's trying to get it. Be careful."

She strolls right past me. I scratch my jaw as I watch her walk through the revolving glass doors.

CHAPTER SIX

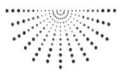

ROBERT TANGO

*E*lise Stein is a lot younger than her name suggests. She's like one of those women who work at *Elle* or *Vogue*. She resembles an Afghan hound with her long, thin, pointy face and bone-straight blond hair.

We're in a lounge, sitting in oversized, red-tufted armchairs. A Latin jazz number is playing lightly in the background, and just about every seat is filled. By the look of it, a lot of deals are being casually made in this room. The longer I hear Elise talk in detail about all the people she knows who are associated with the Atlantic Metropolitan Library Project, the more I'm ready to make a deal of my own.

"So, Robert, tell me more about yourself." She

comes closer. "And not all that tabloid shit that's written about you."

I lean back and cross my foot over my knee. "I've been successful and will continue to be so."

"You're prime choice on the West Coast, but taking the Kennedy out of your name doesn't benefit you on this side of the universe."

I force myself to not look at Grace. The fact that she hasn't cut in and redirected this line of questioning speaks volumes. Instead, I glance at Hannah, who winks at me.

Elise seems to have seen that. She waves her finger between Hannah and me. "So how do you two know each other?"

"We have a mutual friend," Hannah says before I can.

"You know Jack Lord, don't you?"

Elise raises her eyebrows as she straightens her posture. "I know Jack. Well… not personally, but I know of him."

"Also, Hannah and I have worked with each other on a few *major* projects," Grace chimes in.

It doesn't take a rocket scientist to realize she's trying to arouse Elise's curiosity.

I grin at Elise with purpose, and her skin flushes.

"Jack and I were business partners, and his cousin is married to my best friend, who's also my former business partner. Actually, I'm contracted with Lord Development and Construction for East Coast projects."

Her hand flies to her chest. "Is that so?" Elise flashes Grace a quick frown.

Grace shakes her head as if she's stunned. "Well, this is news to me."

I look Grace right in the eye without budging. "Jack and I sealed the deal at the wedding," I lie. The fact that Grace and I seem to be competing for Elise's approval supports Hannah's claim.

Elise's finger shoots up. "Maggie Conroy and Vincent Adams."

I grin, satisfied. "Yes."

"I know someone else who attended that wedding, a first cousin."

I glance at Hannah to acknowledge her smirk. I figured this whole situation was on the way to getting sticky because of Carter and me, but I didn't think I would fall into the sap this fast.

"I assume you're referring to Carter Remington?"

"Yes. Carter's with Metropolis and used to be with Kennedy Creative before you took over."

"She worked with me for a while. But my team is very talented," I say.

"And so is she."

I agree, but I don't say it out loud. Instead, I smile passively.

After a few seconds, Elise takes the hint. She sighs. "Well, here's the issue. I have historically partnered with Metropolis, but—"

Grace holds up a hand to halt her. "I'll explain if you don't mind."

"I mind," I say. "Please continue, Elise?"

Elise's eyes shift between Grace and me. "Are you two partners?"

"How do you mean?" Grace asks.

Elise scoffs. "What other kind of partners are there?"

"Grace runs the interior-design arm of *my* company." I bet Grace is grimacing, but instead of looking to confirm it, I lean closer to Elise, giving her my complete attention. "But I would like to hear you tell me more about my chances of winning this account."

Her face turns red, and she clears her throat. "Okay, well, Stuart..."

"Stuart Beatty?"

She nods once. "Right. He's burned a bridge

with Tom Roth."

I sit back. "Is it an irreparable bridge?"

"Doesn't matter," Grace says.

That's her stab at winning back the floor, and if she believes that having a small opening for Beatty to weasel his way back into Roth's good graces *doesn't matter*, then she's not as formidable as I thought she was.

"So what happened?" Hannah asks out of the blue. I want to grab her and kiss her on the cheek for asking the question that I would have to find a roundabout way to ask.

Elise makes a flippant gesture with her hand. "Money of course."

That's all I need to know. From that point on, Elise wants to hear more about my relationship with Vince and how I made the change from media to architecture. About forty-five minutes into the conversation, Grace checks her watch and reminds Elise that she only had fifty minutes to give us.

"That was only if I didn't like him. I like him," she proclaims, winking at me.

Elise orders another round of drinks, and Grace announces that she has to go to a meeting but she'll join us for breakfast tomorrow. I'm curious about where the hell she's going, but I don't question her because our partnership already nearly unraveled before Elise's eyes, and I need Elise to believe we're still a united front. So when Grace stands, I get up and walk her out of the room.

"What the hell was that?" Grace asks along the way.

"That's what I want to ask you."

"And what's that shit you pulled with Lord Development?"

"It's the truth."

"Well, it doesn't look good when I don't know the truth." She twists her face bitterly. "Us being partners and all."

"But we're not partners. You're my employee."

Grace breathes in sharply and then shakes her head. "Remember that I'm the reason we're here in the first place."

It takes every ounce of self-restraint to keep from lambasting her for being sly. Now I can see it all over her face and even in the way she's carrying herself. Grace isn't the kind of person who loses graciously. I recall how she grilled me at the dinner table the night I came to see her father about buying his company. I get it now. She was trying to locate the weakest buyer, one she could run and rule and have her way with—someone who couldn't detect her slithering up from behind and striking him or her in the neck with her poisonous tongue. I guess I fit the bill since I was known as a womanizer. But that's not the part of me that has shown Grace a lot of *grace*. She benefitted from the part of me that empathizes with the outcasts.

"Who are you meeting with?" I ask since we no longer have to play phony.

She grunts facetiously and stops in her tracks. "Old friends, Robert. What—you don't trust me anymore?"

I look her dead in the eyes. "Of course I trust you, Grace."

"Well, then act like it because whatever's going on between you and Hannah, I feel as if it's a betrayal to me." She jabs herself in the chest. "I liked it better when you were only fucking Carter."

Out of nowhere, Carter and a guy walk right toward us. Grace and I go rigid. Carter is watching us with a peculiar look on her face. I detect surprise, anger, and probably a sense of betrayal.

Grace grunts bitterly as Carter and her date keep moving forward at a casual pace.

"Great." Grace storms away, putting some distance between her and them.

Carter stops and shakes her head. I want her to

glance over at me, but she doesn't. I'm positive she heard the comment Grace made suggesting Hannah and I were fucking. My arms hang as I turn to watch Carter walk out the front door. The guy following her is about my height with dark, curly hair and a trimmed beard. I didn't even know she would be back in DC today.

Now that she's out of sight, I pull myself together with a sigh and head back to join Hannah and Elise. The two women go into a long story about how they first met in St. Barthes and run down a list of people they both know. As they talk, I can't banish thoughts of Carter getting it on with the bearded guy. Every now and then, Elise asks if I know a particular person. Sometimes I say yes. Most of the people on their mutual list know me but not the other way around. And Elise makes a point of focusing on those relationships, recounting where the individuals met me and what I was doing at the time. The stories always have two things in common—I was partying and I was high. It doesn't take me long to figure out why Elise has chosen to spend more time with me.

I take the ants out of my pants and banish my last thought of Carter sucking air in ecstasy while her date tastes her clit. I'm itching to call her to figure out if I have to clarify shit but can't until I conclude this meeting with Elise Stein.

I lean toward Elise and wait. When I have her complete attention, I say, "I didn't get my company on the WPM 500 list by being a party animal and a drug addict. Now, I take it you've been vetting me, and I admire your manner. I like subtlety—it's a classy trait."

Elise sits up straight. "Now, that's something we have in common. And I was vetting you, and you passed with flying colors."

I sit back and steeple my hands in front of me. "And so have you."

She pauses before reaching beside her to retrieve a small purse with studs on it. "Then tonight I'll take a better look at the plans. I'll let Tom know what I think and then follow up with you." She stands, and Hannah and I rise to our feet to meet her. "Will you be attending the dinner tomorrow night?"

"Dinner with Tom Roth?" I ask.

She nods crisply. "In the flesh."

"Then I believe so." I shrug one shoulder. "Grace made the plans."

Elise studies my expression and then sniffs as though she's just been struck by a thought. She opens her purse, takes a business card and a pen, and writes. "Tomorrow night at seven thirty."

I take the card from her and turn it over. There's a Bethesda, Maryland address on the back.

I smirk. "I'll be there."

She winks at me and then gives Hannah a hug as they say good-bye.

"Robert, I would hug you too, but my husband would not approve of me getting so close to all of this that you are," she says, waving her hands in front of me.

I hold out my hand. "Sounds fair."

We shake hands firmly, and then I guide her in for a side hug. "I'm sure he won't lose his lunch over just one."

Elise giggles like a schoolgirl. "I guess not."

I let her go, and she smooths the side of her head. "See you both tomorrow night."

Her skin has turned red, and she seems dazed as she walks out. Hannah and I watch her until she's out of sight.

Hannah pats my arm. "Another one bites the dust."

I frown, confused.

"You, Tango. When a woman fantasizes, it's about fucking you."

We plop back down in our seats.

"That's ridiculous," I say. Women fantasize about men like Vince, not me.

Hannah scoffs and then leans forward, resting her elbows on her thighs. "Tango, you've gotten me off at least twenty times already."

I'm lost for words. Does she want to make her fantasies a reality? I can't help her with that. Not yet. Not with her. Since we're in the same town, I want Carter—tonight. The sooner I can make this happen, the better.

I point my head toward the bar. "I'll get the bill squared away."

"You do that," Hannah says, gazing at me seductively.

I snicker and shake my head. "Snap out of it, Rossi."

She laughs. "One day I will."

I laugh as I trot off to settle our tab.

CHAPTER SEVEN

CARTER REMINGTON

bus passed close enough to rattle the awnings as Carter turned to look through the window of the Iron Stallion on NW Fifty-Eighth Street. She wanted to regurgitate the red wine and crab cakes she'd just consumed when she saw Hannah Rossi and the empty seat with the man's suit coat laid over the chair. Robert was in town with the woman who'd tried all weekend to get his attention. Hell, she'd even knocked on his door in the middle of the night to offer herself to him. Not many men could withstand a sexual charge from the likes of Hannah Rossi, especially Robert Tango. The thought infuriated Carter so much that she almost wished last night with Robert had never happened.

"Who was that?" Rico Denton asked with his hands shoved in his pockets.

"You mean the woman in the chair?"

He shook his head. "In what chair? I'm referring to the woman in the lobby."

Carter grimaced. "Grace?"

"Yeah. Do you know her?"

"Well, yeah, I said her name, so I guess I know her."

"Is she single?" he asked.

"More than likely. What man can stand her?"

Carter was already irritated by where their conversation was going. She had no romantic feelings whatsoever for Rico. Sure, in Denver she'd wanted to make Robert believe she was seeing someone, Rico in particular, but the truth was, after the first date, she and Rico had figured out they were better off as work colleagues and friends. But he was a nice guy, other than being a little too caught up in the political world. He was a drafter who'd wanted to become a senator so much that he quit his job at the firm to take a pay cut and a demotion and work for Hubert Riley, a representative from his home state of New York. Friday was his last day. The office had a big going-away party for him. Since Carter had flown in from Colorado that morning in order to be at work on Monday, she'd made plans to buy Rico a farewell drink. Never in a million years did she expect to run into Robert Tango in downtown DC on a Sunday night, and with Grace and Hannah.

"I don't know… she's hot," Rico said with a shrug.

Carter turned to Rico, attempting to focus on his face as the two names kept playing over and over in her head. Grace and Hannah.

"Unless she's with the guy," he said.

"The guy?" It took a moment to compute. "Robert? No, they're not together. That I know for sure."

Rico thumbed over his shoulder as they turned into the parking garage. "That was *the* Robert Tango?"

"In the flesh," she said cynically.

"You worked for him, didn't you?"

They were only about five feet from his car. It beeped as Rico opened the doors remotely.

"Yes," Carter said curtly, peeling off to the passenger side. Rico hadn't opened the door for her since the first night they went on a date.

They got into the car. Rico looked over at her. "Why are you angry?"

Carter glanced down and unfolded her arms. "I'm not," she said in a fake, high-pitched tone.

"Do you have something going on with Robert Tango?"

Carter pulled back. "No." She knew she sounded like she was lying. "He's my cousin's best friend. So I know him, but that's it." She looked straight ahead and then turned to meet Rico's probing eyes.

He chuckled. "Fine then. But the woman he was with—I want to get to know her. Could you make that happen?"

Carter snarled and folded her arms again. "No," she said as if he were asking her to eat a worm.

"Come on, Carter. I think she's the one."

"What?" she said with a laugh. "I think you've had too many of those screwdrivers. Plus, she's not a friend of mine, so I can't help you."

Rico nodded as if in contemplation. "I sort of got that." He turned on the engine, backed out of the parking spot, and stopped. "Are you saying that this Grace woman is a bitch?"

"The queen of them," Carter replied in a tone meant to convince him of the truth of her words.

"And she doesn't have a boyfriend?"

"I doubt it. She did fuck my ex for a while, but he was ambitious, and she was the boss's daughter."

"Then she's bitter about being used."

"Very."

"I can help her with her condition, you know."

Carter frowned so hard her brain ached. "And I care why?"

"Because, she'll be nice once she's fucked real good."

"Ugh." Carter grunted, disgusted. "Just take me home, please."

"Just think about it."

She turned her narrow eyes on Rico, and he winked.

Carter stabbed her finger toward the front window. "Now. Drive."

The car moved out of the parking ramp. She couldn't believe how sour she was at the moment. Her heart felt so betrayed. She knew why Grace would be in DC with Robert, but what in the hell was Hannah doing there? On the short ride back to her apartment, she fought the urge to call Robert and insist that he answer some questions. Then she thought better of it. Heck, he was more than she could ever expect in a man anyway. He was for Victoria's Secret and *Sports Illustrated* models, not for a confused Californian in-country expatriate like her. Truthfully, she was just an uptight architect who always had to prove she was a woman because she looked way too young for her age. That was why she wore the pixie haircut—it made her look sophisticated enough to be taken seriously and let in the door. However, getting two feet in the door wasn't enough for Carter. She wanted to own the room. One day she would, but for the moment, she was at the bottom of the totem pole, climbing her way to the top.

"Hey, if I upset you by asking about Grace, then…"

She wiggled her head fervently. "You didn't."

"Then why are you quiet?"

"It's work," she said, not wanting to explain the depths of her mood to Rico.

"Or is it Robert Tango?"

Round the next corner and a few blocks up R Street, and she would be home.

"No, it isn't."

"You're lying. You have something going with him."

"I don't, and if I did, I wouldn't tell you."

He grunted thoughtfully. "I guess I wouldn't tell

me either. Since then I would use the info to black-mail you into introducing me to Grace."

Carter studied his large smile. Rico's looks were certainly flawless. Also, he had a dry, cynical, cutting-edge sense of humor like hers, and she knew when he wasn't being serious.

Rico's car stopped in front of her house. Instead of getting out, she turned to face him. "If you want to meet Grace, then I'll set it up."

He beamed. "Really? Cool!"

Carter pointed her finger at him. "But when she rips your head off and eats you alive like a female praying mantis, you cannot hold it against me. Consider yourself warned."

"Got it," he said with way too much enthusiasm.

She wagged her head like a dog's tail. "You have no idea what you're getting yourself into, but to each his own."

Rico wiggled his eyebrows and laughed as Carter opened the door and got out. As soon as her feet hit the concrete, she turned around. "I'll call you and let you know how far I get."

He shot a finger at her. "You better."

Carter closed the car door and nearly skipped all the way up the stairs to her three-story duplex.

The lightness in her steps changed once she realized she'd be sleeping alone that night and Robert would be giving Hannah just what she'd been wanting. Carter growled as she inserted the key into the lock and turned it.

"Oh, oh..." Mrs. Morris, her neighbor, said from inside of her townhome.

Carter quickly assessed whether she could make it inside fast enough. Her hand was on the knob, and Mrs. Morris had already unlatched the last of three locks. Boy, she moved quickly for an eighty-three-year-old lady. If Carter hurried to pull open the door, her neighbor would know that she was trying to escape having a conversation with her.

Mrs. Morris's door opened, and keeping one hand on the doorknob, Carter looked over her shoulder to see the woman.

"Are you okay out here, darling?" Mrs. Morris asked.

Suddenly, Carter's forced smile turned into a real one. "Yep. Everything's fine, Mrs. Morris."

It was always the same. After one look, she regretted wanting to escape her. The need to flee had nothing to do with the woman herself—Carter was always so busy with work that it was hard to slow down and share a few moments with her colorful neighbor.

The eighty-three-year-old was widowed in real life but, according to her, not in reality. That night, she wore a white scarf around her head with a big bow in the front and a crocheted red rose in the center and big black horn-rimmed glasses. As usual, her face was made up, and she wore a frilly, short-sleeved blousy rose-patterned dress.

"Well, that's good to hear, darling."

Carter turned all the way around to face her. Her smile broadened. "How are you doing this evening?"

Mrs. Morris's smile faded, and she spaced out. Carter knew exactly what was happening.

"Is Mr. Morris still around?" Carter asked.

Mrs. Morris snickered. "Oh dear, you think I'm an old crackpot." She studied Carter with one eye narrowed. "You've been with your beau recently, haven't you?"

Carter rolled her eyes involuntarily. Mrs. Morris was always spying on her by looking out the window. "I've told you twice already that Rico isn't my beau. We're just friends."

Her elderly neighbor chuckled flightily. "Oh no,

darling, not the nice young gentleman who wants to be president of the United States one day."

Carter's mouth fell open. *How can she know about Rico's political aspirations if she hasn't spoken to him?* "Have you ever spoken to Rico?"

"No, dear, I've already said. I have gifts."

Carter recalled the woman saying that on a number of occasions, but she'd always chalked it up to Mrs. Morris being bored, lonely, and little kooky.

Carter took a step back. It was still hard to believe this eccentric elderly woman had some sort of sixth sense. "You must've spoken to Rico at some point. He tells everyone who will listen that he wants to be a senator."

Mrs. Morris stepped closer to Carter, took her hand, and patted the top of it. "But I said 'president.'"

Carter gulped. It was as if her head were leaving her body. "Right," she barely said.

"Your beau. You were together." Mrs. Morris let go of Carter's hand to thoughtfully put her finger on her lip. "After a wedding."

Carter remained lost for words.

Mrs. Morris gazed off as she did when she was receiving messages from her imaginary dead husband. "I'm coming in now, my love," she called over her shoulder. "Victor doesn't like it when I'm out of the house this late."

Carter's first instinct was always to placate her, but now she didn't know what to think. Perhaps Mrs. Morris did have some sort of connection with the unknown.

"I must head in, dear."

Carter nodded stiffly. "Sure. Good night." As usual, she waited for Mrs. Morris to go inside first.

The woman opened the door and then quickly faced Carter. "He is your true love."

"Who?" Carter couldn't move a muscle.

"The handsome fellow you made love to." Mrs. Morris beamed as she went inside and closed herself in for the night with her ghost. Carter instantly felt a chill of fear. Could there be such a thing as husbands who couldn't die and a woman who could identify someone's one true love? She never believed in stuff like that, and she didn't want to start.

Carter shook her head in an effort to reset her acceptance of what was possible and what was not. As soon as she entered her place, jet lag hit her with a crushing blow to the head. After adjusting the air-conditioning to even out the humidity, she stripped off her clothes and underwear until she was naked, turned off the lights, switched on the TV to watch a recording of *The Good Daughter,* and crawled into bed.

Images of Robert Tango played through her mind—him standing in the foyer of the bar, watching her pass by, and him shifting his rigid cock in and out of her slipperiness the way he had the night before. Gosh, she was so wet. She loved the way he sucked on her neck as though he wanted to eat her alive and the swirl of orgasm igniting her pussy when he went down on her. She realized there was so much more to his appeal than mere sex, but the fact that she loved the way he stared at her and sexed her made it difficult to remember his great personality.

Then she remembered what Mrs. Morris had said. Could Robert Tango be her one true love? Her cell phone rang in her purse, and she kicked off the covers and rushed over to the dresser by the window to see who was calling. She gasped when she saw the initials RT on her screen.

CHAPTER EIGHT

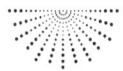

ROBERT TANGO

She says, "Hello," and I stop pacing.

"Hey, Carter," I say, feeling jumpy.

"Hi, Robert."

There's awkward silence between us. I don't know what to say to her, but at the same time, I have a lot to say.

"Um, sorry about earlier." I squeeze my eyes shut, regretting the words as soon as they leave my mouth. What the hell am I apologizing for?

"What did you do earlier that you need to apologize for?" she asks right on cue. That's another reason why I like her—she's sharp.

"I should've told you I'd be in DC."

"Why are you here?"

I crack a tiny smile. "Are you grilling me?"

"You started with the apology."

I can feel her smiling on the other side of the phone. I chuckle. "You had a date tonight, I see." Hell, seeing her with that guy stung, and not a little.

"Yeah… well…"

"Well what?" I ask, wanting her to explain how she could go out with another guy so soon after what we did together. That's the sort of shit I used to do when I was more broken than I am now.

"He's just a friend," she says as though she's not convinced of it.

"A friend with benefits?"

"Nope. I took him out for drinks tonight since I missed his going-away party on Friday. But was that Hannah I saw in the Iron Stallion?"

Good. She's jealous. "Yes."

"Are you traveling with her?"

"Yes, but only for business."

She snorts.

"What? You don't believe me?"

"I believe you, but it's her I don't believe. She's not going to stop until you pay attention."

I walk to the window to take in the view of the city. Carter is somewhere out there on the phone, talking to me. I want her in this room, standing next to me, preferably with her clothes off.

"Carter?" I say in a calm voice

"Yes?" She sounds highly intrigued.

"I don't want her. I want you. I want you now, but we both have to work tomorrow."

"Is that why you're in town—for work?"

I grin. "Yes."

"The Metropolitan Atlantic Library Project?"

"That's why Hannah is in town. She's working with Grace on the interior-design portion."

"But… never mind."

"But what?"

"Forget it."

We fall silent again. I'm aware that Carter is the competition. She's a formidable opponent, and I'm pretty sure she knows that Elise Stein has been contracted to handle interior design.

"Listen," I say in a tone that redirects our conversation. "How about I take you to lunch tomorrow?"

"Can't," she quickly says. "How about dinner instead?"

I smirk. "Can't."

"Really?" She sounds genuinely interested. "Are you having a special dinner with someone tomorrow night?"

"Nope. I have plans. As you know, I am in town for one—now two—reasons."

"I know the one, but what's the second?"

"You. I want to be with you, Carter." Just saying it makes my heart beat like thunder.

She's quiet, and my heart is still going.

"Hello?" I say.

"Why don't *you* let *me* take you out on Tuesday night?" Carter says.

Shit, I have a big grin pasted on my face. "Yeah?"

"Yeah."

"Okay then."

Once again, it's silent between us. I go sit on the side of the bed and unbutton my shirt.

"So what are you doing now?" I ask.

"Watching TV."

"Oh yeah? What are you watching?"

"*The Good Daughter.*"

I grunt as I take my shirt off. "Never heard of it."

"Well, I'm about to turn it off and go to sleep now," she says and then yawns.

"Are you in bed?" Shit, my dick is getting firm.

"I am," she croons.

"Alone?"

"All alone."

I grin. She's flirting with me, and it's working. "How far are you from the Continental on the River Hotel?"

"Not far…"

I'm propelled to my feet by excitement. "How about I come over?"

She chuckles. "How about we see each other on Tuesday?"

Shit. I want to explode. "You can wait that long?"

"Barely." She yawns.

"It's late," I say, conceding.

Carter drags out a sigh. "Yeah."

It's taking every bit of willpower to not push it. I would be okay sleeping next to her, but the moment she pins her sweet ass to my dick, there's no stopping what would happen next.

"Then I'll see you on Tuesday. Why don't you text me your address?"

Without delay, my phone buzzes. She's had her address already locked and loaded, which means she must've given some serious consideration to my offer.

"There you go," she says.

Damn. I don't want to let her go, but my head is

spinning because I'm jet-lagged and so turned on right now. "Then I'll see you soon?"

"Okay."

The line falls silent, and I can hear her breathing. After long moment I say, "Good night, Carter."

"Good night, Robert."

I wait until she ends the call, and after a few beats, she does.

I'm rejuvenated as I strip down and get in bed. As soon as I turn off the lights, my cell phone rings again. I answer quickly, knowing that it's Carter.

"Hi," I say in a seductive tone.

"Meet me for breakfast in the Riverside Inn, here in the hotel, at nine," Grace says and then hangs up.

After a moment, I sigh and set my phone on the nightstand. That was a fucking buzz kill. Another buzz kill will be to have Hannah knocking on my door the moment she gets horny. She promised she wouldn't, but I don't buy it. Hannah's too much of the person I used to be. I look at the door. It's locked and dead bolted. I put the room phone on silent mode. I turn the ringer off on my cell phone and set my alarm clock to go off at seven in the morning. I have some calls to make before breakfast with Grace.

The blackout shades are lowered, and the lights are out, and a few minutes later, I'm in bed and fall sound asleep.

"SHIT…" MY HEAD IS GROGGY AS I SLAP AT THE nightstand for my phone. It's buzzing loudly, and I'm the only one who can stop it. Finally, I get it in my hands and swipe the screen to turn it off.

"Fuck…" I sit on the side of the bed, rubbing my eyes until they focus better in the dusky room. These days, I'm not big on wasting minutes. I leap to my feet and use the remote to open the shades. The sky is gray and the light murky. Some might consider the current conditions a mood killer, but I thrive on these cruddy East Coast days.

I smack my tongue, tasting morning breath and yesterday's drinks with Elise Stein. I go to the bathroom to brush my teeth and shower. That takes fifteen minutes. As soon as I'm out, I dry off and put on my pajama bottoms and a robe.

My thoughts are clearer after that. I sit at the desk and place my first call to my lawyer, Richard Darling. He's shrewd, and knows where to find the difficult information I need.

"Hello, Robert," Richard says after the third ring.

"Morning, Richard. About Grace Kennedy. I think she's trying to raise Kennedy Creative out of the ashes. Could you look into it?"

"I'll do some digging, but don't worry—there's no way she can reprise Kennedy Creative. You own the name. If she does try it, then we'll be ready for it, and Ralph Kennedy will be in breach of contract. He'll have to pay penalties upward of fifty percent of the purchase price, plus she'll need your permission to authenticate the business."

I shake my head thoughtfully. I'm pretty sure Grace knows this. "She has to be up to something."

"Like I said, I'll look into it."

"What about Kennedy Creative Interior? What if I want to dissolve the contract I made with her?"

He pauses. I can feel him thinking. "There are ways, but unless she's operating at a consecutive six months' loss of thirty-five percent or more, you're going to have to pay."

"How much?"

"I have to crunch the numbers, but I estimate at least seven million. Although…"

"What is it?"

"There's a clause that says she can terminate the contract at will."

I shake my finger. "Yes, that's right. I figured I'd give her an out if she felt she couldn't handle the workload." I nod thoughtfully. "She's not going to quit if she can collect that much money."

"I doubt it."

"Okay, thanks. I look forward to hearing from you."

"I'll get back to you soon," he says.

We hang up, and I call Gabe Zenith, my accountant, and ask him to generate a monthly profit-loss report for KCID, starting from the point of inception until now. He says he'll have the reports sent to me by messenger within the next twenty-four hours. The last call I make is to Zoe to go over important action items, my calendar for the next month, and the project reports. I also give her the green light to start interviewing second and third assistants.

As soon as we hang up, someone rattles my door.

"Who is it?"

"It's me, Hannah," she says, controlling her tone.

I look down at myself. "I'll meet you at breakfast in fifteen."

"Breakfast?" she says as though this is the first time she's hearing about it.

I shuffle to the door, unlock the bolt, and open it. "Breakfast, nine o'clock, Riverside Inn?"

Hannah touches her face as she stares at me with a blank expression.

I frown, concerned. "Are you okay?"

She wiggles her head. "Um, yeah. It's just—fuck, Tango, you're like a *GQ* ad."

I sigh hard. "Come on, Rossi, I thought we were beyond the high-school-crush shit."

"We are." She sweeps past me and into my room. "But you're still hot."

I close the door. "Here's where my expertise comes into play—wanting someone because they're hot never makes a relationship work."

She flops down on my bed and spreads her long legs. I notice her pussy in the tight black pants she's wearing. Hannah has serious style, and it shows in the clothes she wears. Not many women can make sexy not look slutty, and she's one of them.

"Damn it, Tango. I wish I got my hands on you before you found religion."

I chuckle as I look away from her. There was a

time when I would nearly hyperventilate, having someone as desirable as Hannah spreading her legs while sitting on my bed, displaying what she's willing to give me. I would've ripped her pants off and fucked her into tomorrow. But after noticing her pleasant crotch, all I can think about is jeopardizing what I have with Carter as well as messing up what I could have with Hannah in the form of our interior-design division. Basically, I'm no longer in the business of fucking without considering the consequences.

"Okay, so why the visit?" I ask, getting us back on track.

"Why wasn't I invited to breakfast?"

"You are now."

"But Grace told me there's no breakfast this morning and said I'm to meet her at Elise's office at two p.m. So now I'm meeting with a client in Alexandria this morning."

There's something fishy going on here, and I don't like it one bit that Grace is calling all the shots.

I calmly sit down beside Hannah. "Listen, how well do you *really* know Elise?"

Hannah crosses her legs and sits up straight. "Pretty well. We go back a long away."

"How long?"

She shrugs. "Nine, ten years. She used to design runway stages before she discovered interior design."

Suddenly, a lightbulb turns on in my head. "And what about Grace? How well do you *really* know her?"

Hannah uncrosses her legs and shrugs as though my line of questioning is making her nervous. "I don't know—three, four years, and we're not really that close."

Regardless of her discomfort, I forge ahead. "Are you closer to Elise than she is?"

"Yes. Definitely. I…" She stops. Her eyes have grown wide, like a child caught with her hand in the cookie jar.

Knowing the part of Hannah's behavior that may be the reason she's sitting next to me now, I wink at her to put her at ease. "Let me guess. You called Grace once you heard I was interested in the library project and hooked her up with Elise."

"Well, close."

I shrug, gesturing for her to explain.

Hannah explains how everyone who's in interior design has heard of the Metropolitan Atlantic Library Project. On Friday evening, the day before the wedding, she overhead Carter mention being in competition with RT Design in trying to land the account—for the interior and the structure. Even before she ran into me at the wedding, she knew that the Elise Stein Agency was already contracted as the interior designer. Since Hannah was looking to break into interior design and get to know me better, she called Grace and made a deal with her. If we put her on the project, she will be able to get her subcontracted with Elise Stein.

"And you're the one who knew about Stuart Beatty burning his bridge with Tom Roth," Hannah said. "Elise knew, and she let me know that there still could be an in for your company. However, Beatty is willing to kiss some major ass to land that project, so watch out."

Suddenly, my head branches off in three different directions. I didn't come all this way to lose that contract. I also wonder what sort of game Grace is playing. And finally, I want to know if Hannah is willing to help me kill two buzzards with one stone.

"Listen, Rossi, I have a proposition for you. You want to hear it?"

She smirks. "I've been waiting for you to say those words."

CHAPTER NINE

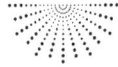

ROBERT TANGO

J ride down the elevator on my way to the Riverside Inn Café. I feel so damn good, knowing no matter what, I'm in a great position to outsmart Grace at whatever game she's playing. After stepping out of the elevator, I move to the side so the others riding down with me can pass, and I tap out a text message.

"Good morning, beautiful. Can't wait until tomorrow night. I'll call you later."

I send the text to Carter and drop my phone into my briefcase. I don't feel a vibration or hear a chime, which means she hasn't gotten back to me yet. I'm not used to women playing it as cool as Carter. She said the guy she was with only a friend. I don't take her for the lying type, so I believe her. Regardless, I can hardly wait to see her tomorrow night, and hell, I hope she feels the same way.

I get to the door of the restaurant and see Grace sitting by the window, sipping coffee. Since she doesn't see me, I take a moment to study her. I really liked Grace when I asked her to head the interior-design branch, and I thought I was doing her a favor by keeping her family name in the company. I know how it feels to lose everything and how no one gives a damn about it. I gave a damn. If I turn out to be wrong about her kicking me in the balls, then the worst-case scenario—for her, not me—is she'll share the duties of running Kennedy Creative Interior Designs equally with Hannah. However, if Grace is thinking about double-crossing me, then she'll be out on her ass as fast as she can say uncle.

I approach the table, and she turns to look at me. Her miserable expression transforms into a frown of disapproval as she reads the time on her wristwatch.

I sit down. "Good morning."

"You're late."

I tilt my head. "So, not so good morning?"

She blows a hard breath through her nose like a

mad bull. "We don't have time for breakfast, only coffee."

"We or you?"

She grimaces. "Listen, what the fuck is going on between Hannah and you?"

I snort facetiously. "Nothing."

"Are you fucking her?"

"Didn't you ask me that already?"

"Was she in your room this morning?"

I realize that my body has shifted forward, so I sit up and then back in my chair. I catch sight of the waitress and motion to her. I don't take my eyes off the woman as she walks toward our table. I want Grace to sweat.

"Are you ready to order, sir?"

"Yes, I'll have a stack of pancakes, sausages, and black coffee."

The waitress writes that on the pad. "Thank you, sir. And you, ma'am?" She looks at Grace.

"More coffee, that's all."

"Got it. Then I'll just take your menus."

I hand her the unopened menu that's sitting in front of me, and Grace hands over hers too.

Once the waitress is gone, I set my eyes back on Grace. "The answer to your question is no, we're not fucking, nor have I ever fucked Hannah, but who I choose to fuck is none of your fucking business, got it?" I say calmly.

Grace rolls her eyes and then takes a deep breath. "I want you to know that I'm committed to your company, so you don't have to distrust me."

I narrow my eyes. Grace and I can continue to beat around the bush, but I'd rather lead her down a different path. "So how was your time with friends last night?"

She looks me right in the eyes. "Fine. And yours?"

I hesitate, processing her demeanor. Fuck, I would've liked it better if she had looked away because then I would've known she wasn't trying to fuck me over out of bitterness. But the way she's glaring at me—I read defiance.

"I went straight to bed."

"With whom?"

I snort bitterly. "What is your fucking problem?"

She shrugs indifferently. "You're the one with the reputation."

"You're still holding that over me? When have you seen me live up to this fucking mysterious reputation you say I have?"

"Mysterious?"

Again, I have to sit back because the intensity of

our last exchange drove me forward. I sigh. I'm over it. "Okay, what do you want to discuss regarding our dinner with Tom Roth tonight?"

"It's off. You can fly back to San Francisco because Metropolis has the account."

I move back slightly. "And you came across this information somewhere between leaving the bar last night and sitting here this morning?"

She sets her jaw. "Yes."

I snort again and shake my head.

"What?" she asks.

Holy fuck, do I want to lay into her for playing a shabby game of chess, but instead, I smile like a man who's resigned to losing the account, and I drum the table.

"Okay then," I say.

She jerks, taken aback. "Okay?"

"Yes. Okay."

"Okay, so you'll fly back tonight?"

"Yep."

She checks her watch again. "I would too, but I have to go over some plans with Elise. At least half of your company is on the Atlantic Metropolitan Library Project—that's something. Oh, and I already called Hannah to let her know that Elise and I won't be needing her assistance."

I force myself to smile. "All right."

Grace tilts her head and then calmly raises her coffee to her mouth and sips. "I don't believe you."

"What don't you believe?"

"That you're okay with walking away without a fight."

I tilt my head. "Is there a fight to be had?"

"No," she says quickly.

The waitress brings my pancakes, sausage, and coffee. She starts to pour Grace a new cup, but Grace holds up a hand to halt her. "No, thank you." She takes her purse off the back of her chair.

"Don't worry. I'll foot the bill," I say.

Grace smiles, and this time it's genuine. "I know." She winks.

I smirk. "Then have a productive meeting."

"I will." She rises to her feet. "I'll see you back in San Francisco, then?"

"I have business to attend to between here and there, but I'll see you when I see you."

Her phony smile drops. "What kind of business?"

"Business that doesn't involve you."

Grace hesitates. "Well, um, see you."

I nod.

She walks away, and I pick up my fork to tear

into the stack of pancakes. My briefcase buzzes, and I take my smartphone out. Carter replied to my last email. "I hardly come here," she writes with a picture of a quarter of her face in the shot as though she took a selfie while falling. Regardless, I gaze at the piece of her face she sent me. It's a strange shot and response to my earlier text message. She's so pretty. I'm about to tuck the phone back into my bag when something in the background catches my eye.

"Fuck!" I shout.

Those who hear it glare at me.

I'm losing my shit. My fingers are shaking as I hurry up and call Hannah.

"Hello," she says, picking up on the first ring.

"Let's talk."

I WALK INTO A COFFEE SHOP ON S STREET. HANNAH is sitting at a table, waving. I pick up my pace and plop down in the seat across from her.

"You look green, Tango," she says, grimacing.

I hand her my cell phone with the photo Carter sent me on the screen. "Look."

"That's Carter."

"Look behind her. The two guys way in the back at the table."

Hannah's eyebrows furrow. "The older guy and the younger one?"

"Yes. Have you ever met Ralph Kennedy?"

"Once." She garners a closer look. "No, twice." Suddenly she jerks back. "What the fuck? That's Ralph Kennedy."

"Do you recognize who he's sitting with?"

Hannah is still examining the picture. "No. Who is he?"

"Stuart Beatty."

She drops the phone from her face. "Of Metropolis?"

"Yep."

"So he's who Metropolis is using to get back into Tom Roth's good graces?" she asks.

"That's what it looks like."

Hannah frowns at the picture again. "Doesn't Carter work for him?"

I nod. "Yes, she does."

"Why would she send you this? I thought she was on Metropolis's team for the AMLP."

After staring long and hard into Hannah's eyes, I make a sudden movement and scratch the back of my head. "I don't know. I'm going to have to talk to her."

"You should, but before you do that, we should get active."

"I agree."

Hannah holds out her fist, waiting for me to bump it. I'm half-distraught over what might be going on at that table with Ralph and Stuart, but I take a soothing sigh and knock my fist against hers. Hannah keeps her fist pressed against mine.

"I would rather be a part of your company than fuck you, Tango. And you can take that claim to the bank and cash it."

I study her for authenticity. I don't have to look long before I believe her. "Ditto," I say.

CARTER REMINGTON

Carter sat at her desk, wondering if she'd made the right decision in taking that photo of Stuart and Ralph. She was sure Stuart didn't see her. The only reason she went to Bagels & Café was because Stuart raved about their bagels a few months earlier during a staff meeting. Stuart was one of those guys who gave just about every restaurant, café, or bar a low review, so when he raved at Bagels & Café, she knew she had to try what they were selling. That morning when she woke up, mad at herself for not telling Robert what she really wanted—him in her bed, making love to her—she had a craving for a good toasted everything bagel with onion-flavored cream cheese. The establishment was way on the other side of the town, but she chose to be adventurous and ride her motorcycle.

It was after seven in the morning when she found a parking spot near the bagel shop. The place was already lively. As she got off her bike, the first thing she noticed was a black Mercedes Benz that had a license plate that read Metropolis. It was Stuart Beatty's car. She almost got back on her bike and drove away. She didn't really want to run into him. When she'd woken up that morning and dragged her tired body to her computer to scan her emails, she'd found an urgent message from him. He wanted to see her in his office at ten thirty. He didn't say why, but Carter imagined it was because he heard Robert was in town.

Now, she wouldn't have drawn a direct connection between him wanting to meet with her and Robert's appearance in DC if Stuart hadn't asked her a number of times to define her relationship with Robert Tango. He had heard they were close. The only thing she'd told him was that they grew up together because he was her cousin's best friend. Then he grilled her about how close she was to Vincent Adams. She told him about the summer vacations in Sag Harbor and the call and gift she got from Vince every year on her birthday. Stuart even crossed the line and asked what sort of gifts he sent. Carter wanted to say that it wasn't his business, but she really wanted in on the most important accounts, so she'd told him.

Carter stood outside the bagel shop. She couldn't just show up at the door and then drive away without scoring the five-star bagels. She decided to enter cautiously and try everything in her power to avoid being seen by Stuart.

There were enough people between the door and the register to creep inside without being noticed by anyone sitting at the tables. As her probing glare moved deeper into the room, at first she saw Ralph Kennedy, who was facing the window, with Stuart sitting across from him. They were deeply engaged in conversation. Carter had to think fast. It could've been nothing, but she would rather let Robert decide that. So she took a quick shot with her cell phone and ended up leaving without ordering her bagels anyway.

Now it was nine thirty in the morning, and she had just noticed something very peculiar. She had been cc'd on all emails regarding the Atlantic Metropolitan Library Project up until last Thursday. On Friday she had nothing, and this morning still nothing. All of that was different than normal. The team communicated about the plans twenty-four, seven. Even while she was in Denver, she communicated with the team. Was she kicked off the squad? Carter began to construct the timeline in her mind. She remembered making out in the parking lot of the tent rental place with Robert. Grace called and knew she was with him. That was on Thursday, late morning. Carter looked at the time she'd received the last email on the project. It concerned the final schematic of the left wing of the library. She clicked on the attachment and was hit with an "access denied" message.

"Right," she muttered and tapped the butt of her pen on the desk. "Yes."

She took her cell phone out of the breast pocket of her jacket and pulled up the photo of Stuart and Ralph Kennedy. Maybe she was wrong, Stuart and Ralph just happened to be old friends out for what

Stu called "the greatest bagels on earth," and the file she'd just tried to open was merely corrupted.

But the timing had to be more than coincidental. And her instincts told her something wasn't right.

"Ah, just do it," she mumbled.

Carter opened her messenger app to send Robert a text and saw one from him to her: "Good morning, beautiful. Can't wait until tomorrow night. I'll call you later."

She grinned from ear to ear.

"Good news?"

Carter looked up. Stuart was standing in the opening of her cubicle.

Her mouth fell open. She tried not to look as if she'd been caught, so she closed her mouth. "Morning, Stu."

"You're here, I'm here. How about we meet now?"

"Sure," Carter said in a high-pitched voice.

Stuart tapped on the wall of her cubicle. "Okay. Just give me five."

She nodded and waited until he was good and gone to send the photo. Once it was sent, she took a deep breath. There. That felt like the right thing to do. Five minutes later, she headed to Stuart's office.

CHAPTER TEN

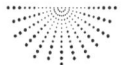

ROBERT TANGO

*I*t's noon, and Zoe confirms that Grace has already called to check whether I booked my flight and, if so, to what city. Just to keep Zoe honest, I asked her to book me on a flight to New York, flying out any time between six and seven in the evening. Grace asked Zoe for my flight details, and I tell her to send them. We need Grace to believe that I'm serious about leaving DC. Hannah and I have checked out of the hotel and are now staying in a six-bedroom, six-bath home in Alexandria, Virginia. We're preparing for the arrival of my team members, who are on the way. Hannah's personal assistant, Sarah, has already flown in from New York to join us. Elise is also here. She's solidly aligned herself with RT Creative, and now she's adjusting her interior-design plans to match our structural design. Sarah has called to have pizza and groceries delivered for at least the next two weeks.

We have just finished fully conceptualizing and designing the lobby of the library.

I rub my eyes.

Elise claps her hands one time. "Well, that was fun."

I check the time on my wristwatch. "It's almost six o'clock."

"Time flies when things are going smoothly," she says.

Hannah gets up. "We better get ready to head out to Tom's."

Elise stands. "I won't be there tonight, but Tom already knows who I want to work with." She shakes her head with a slight eye roll. "He's milking this process for all the attention he can get."

I rise. "So you say there are going to be others at this dinner?"

"You can count on Stuart Beatty being there."

I raise my eyebrows. "What in the world is his objective?"

"His objective is to play the table against each other."

"You mean see who kisses his ass the hardest?" Hannah says.

Elise shakes her head. "No, he's more strategic than that." She starts walking toward the door.

Hannah and I follow.

"Do elaborate," Hannah says.

We make it to the front door. Elise turns to us. "He's searching for the lion."

I smirk. "The strongest."

"Exactly. Whichever of you will not eat his bullshit even though he'll try to force-feed it to you."

"Got it," I say.

"Good luck," Elise says.

Hannah pats me on the back. "He—we—won't need it."

Elise snorts and then grins at us coyly. She shifts her finger between Hannah and me. "The two of you make a handsome couple."

Hannah puts her arm around my neck. "That's what I said when I first saw him. But alas, he's not available."

"No?" Elise sounds intrigued.

Hannah cups a hand against the side of her mouth. "Secret lover."

Elise lifts her eyebrows. "Oh. Woman or man?"

"Kind of a little girl," Hannah says.

Elise's eyes expand as if she's learned something about me that might make her change her mind.

"Oh, it's not what you think. She's in her twenties." Hannah looks at me with her head tilted. "What is she—twenty-four, twenty-five?"

"Darling, that's old enough," Elise says. "Especially for a man as good-looking as Robert."

I wave my hands. "All right, ladies. Enough about my private life."

"But why? I was starting to have fun all over again," Elise says.

I laugh. I like working with people who don't take life so seriously that they can't be humorous. Elise and Hannah are witty.

Hannah and I walk Elise to her car. She wishes us luck, and we hurry inside to prepare for the night. Hannah goes to her room, and I go to mine. However, before I put on a suit, I make a call—one that will give me the leverage I need just in case tonight turns into the blood brawl of the big cats.

HANNAH IS DRESSED TO IMPRESS. SHE'S WEARING A strappy dress that fits her like a glove. It comes down past her knees and is the same color as her skin.

"You look nice tonight," I say as she steps out of the black sedan she rented and hands her keys to the valet.

We decided to take separate cars since she'll have to leave early to style a midnight photo shoot at the Smithsonian. After the shoot, there are supposed to be cocktails and live music. She asked me to stop by after dinner. It'll be fun. Looking at Hannah now, it's clear she's a dangerous one. Her face, body, and humor are all perfect. She's smart and knows how to get what she wants in a diplomatic manner. But I'm unable to crave her the way she deserves to be desired. I'm falling for another woman, and all of Hannah's scrumptiousness can't change that. So I thanked her for inviting me but declined her invitation.

Hannah paws at the air. "I figured the lion needs an alluring lioness."

I snicker and hold my arm out so she can link hers around it.

"So Tango, who would've guessed we'd be doing this together?" she says as we walk up the footpath.

"I certainly couldn't have."

Hannah chuckles. "I bet you think I'm doing all this because I want you."

"Not at all," I say, observing the triangular eaves of the modern contemporary colonial. It's typical that a guy like Tom Roth would live in a place like this. Four redbrick chimneys rise from the massive house, two on each side. A front porch lined with four white columns, also two on each side, pulls double duty by holding up the balcony. Large, double-paned windows run across the ground and second floor. This house has four attic windows bulging out of the rooftop. Just by assessing the property from one end to the other, I can tell there's a swimming pool in the back and tennis courts behind that. I know this kind of guy. I doubt he would build a house without at least those two luxuries.

"No?" Hannah asks, sounding highly curious.

"No. You're successful. You know a good career move when you see it."

Hannah's silent as we get closer to the front door. "Yeah… I'm tired of flying all over creation for the good jobs. I want a more settled life. Cleo's married. Maggie's married now. If I'm never in one place with men who aren't either cheating douche bags or gay, then I'll probably end up an old maid. And let me tell you, Tango, when I first met you…"

"I know. I was a douche bag."

"A double douche. But look at you now."

We make it to the front door, and she turns to face me.

"I mean, am I going to end up like Monroe?" she whispers as if her fear is a secret.

I get the underbelly of disdain the two women have for each other. Theirs is a friendship that probably lasted five years too long. Maggie and Cleo seem to be the glue holding those two together. But the more I've learned about Monroe, the more interesting she has become.

"That wouldn't be such a bad thing. Monroe is bold, and so are you. Here's my advice to you: keep living without forcing it, and before you know it, bam."

The corners of her mouth turn down. "What's bam?"

"Bam is all the good shit that life has in store for you."

Hannah's frown steadily turns upside down. "Damn it, Tango. And you're sure you're not interested in me?"

"Believe me, Hannah, I'm not what you need."

"Carter's what you need?"

I could ignore the look she's giving me, or I could address it. Hannah's been instrumental in getting me this far. After my talk with Jack earlier, I may not even need anyone who will be sitting at the dinner table tonight. I prefer it that way. Jack is going to get back in touch with me as soon as he can. He's aware that I'm at this dinner and what I'm seeking to accomplish. What I have on my side is his disdain for Tom Roth. They've had some run-ins, which Jack's not willing to elaborate on. He would only say that the guy is all brawn with no follow-through. However, deep down I know Hannah has helped me get this far because she wants a romantic relationship with me. I've convinced myself that it's opportunity she seeks, and so has she—but we both know that's not the full truth.

"Maybe." I now see an extra glimmer of hope in Hannah's eyes. "I mean yes. I have feelings for Carter."

Hannah's posture stiffens. Jeez, I might've just broken her heart and risked losing her support. She turns her glassy eyes to the door and rings the bell. I watch her as it chimes. What can I say? What should I say?

After a few anxious seconds, Tom Roth, the man I never met in person but recognize from countless photos, opens the door.

"Good evening," he says and invites us in.

Hannah and I exchange the appropriate greetings and enter, and she's back in good spirits.

The sounds of our footsteps echo as we walk on the white marble floor. I'm looking around as Hannah engages him in small talk about his wife and twin daughters, who are now seven years old. A man's house can say a lot about him. I wouldn't have thought Tom Roth had any kids by the way the house is designed. The floor plan is wide open with high walls and ceilings. There's a grand piano next to an electric fireplace. The furniture is white velvet, and there are abstract oil paintings on the walls. In the middle of the floor is a large white sheepskin rug. On it sits a square glass coffee table with an intricately decorated top piece. The fact that he keeps his house this way says two things: he rules the roost, and his seven-year-old daughters know to keep their hands off his pristine shit.

"So Amy isn't here?" Hannah asks.

"She and the girls are in California with her sister for a few days." He extends his hand toward me. "You must be Robert Tango."

I take a better look at Tom Roth. He looks younger in real life, perhaps in his mid to late thirties. His hair is on the verge of graying, and although he has youthful, close-set eyes, he looks as though he gets put through the ringer on a daily basis.

I shake his hand. "Yes, and thank you for inviting me to your home."

"You've come a long way from San Francisco to sit at my table. I hope the cook makes it worth your while."

I grin crookedly. Let the fucking games begin.

Suddenly, I hear a woman laugh, and I recognize the voice. I've had to learn the sound because every time she's near, I'm forced to prepare myself for the controversy she brings with her.

"It seems everybody's here," Tom says.

"Are we late?" Hannah asks.

"No, you're not. The others arrived early. Grace Kennedy said something about the early bird catching the worm." He winks at her.

This guy is already feeling the power of pitting one of us against the other, but considering the call I made before coming here, there's a strong chance that I will knock the king off the throne.

"So Grace is here?" I say.

"Yes, sure."

"With Ralph Kennedy?"

Hannah shoots me a look of warning.

He scratches the back of his neck nervously. "How about you follow me."

I nod and step aside so that Hannah can walk directly behind him. Already, the evening is shaping up to be a doozy. We walk through a dim-lit hallway that has a glass-domed roof. It's a nice touch, and if Tom hadn't been such a dick so far, I would compliment him on it. I can see the light shining from the room we're approaching, and Grace's voice is coming in clearer.

"Stuart must really put a lot of trust in you," she says, but no one answers.

As soon as we make it to the dining room, I see why she doesn't get a response. She's speaking to Carter, who's sitting at the table. I lock eyes with Carter for a moment, and then she studies Hannah. It's apparent she doesn't like the sight of us together, and I feel a profound need to explain once again that it's only business between us.

However, I can't look at her too long because the person I hoped not to see tonight is also present. "Ralph. Didn't expect to see you here," I say before Grace can speak.

Ralph turns to Grace with a "what next?" expression on his face.

"Have a seat." Tom plops down in the chair at the head of the table.

It's almost laughable, and I so fucking hope that Jack comes through. Suddenly, my cell phone in my pants pocket vibrates. That has to be Jack, and right on time.

"Father and Tom are old friends," Grace says. "They've worked together on numerous projects, so it's natural that Tom would ask Father to be here tonight."

My frown is so severe that my head hurts. I grunt facetiously. "I see." I then take the phone out of my pocket.

"I wanted all factions here tonight because I'll be making my final decision tomorrow and tying up the final contract with AMLP," Tom says. "Excuse me, Tango, is there something more important on your cell phone?"

I raise a finger and keep on reading. Jack wrote, "The deal's on. I have AMLP, and you're my architect. Good to be back in business."

My lips stretch into a slow smile. It's time to have some fun. "Sorry, *Roth*." I put the phone back in my pocket.

Tom stretches his neck as if my actions and tone made it tight. "No problem," he says although by the look on his face, he doesn't mean it.

A woman in a chef's hat comes out, and Tom gives this long-winded introduction of where she works and how long she's been cooking and her specialty. Instead of paying attention to him, my gaze rests on Carter. She's sexier than I've ever seen her in a scarlet dress that matches her lipstick. Why did she come to dinner dressed like a siren? I smirk at her, and she looks away as though embarrassed.

Now the chef is naming the first course: cold split-pea and ginger-mint soup with crusted garlic bread.

"Thank you, Chef Detrick," Tom says.

Chef Detrick bows out of the room.

"So, Robert. I heard it's been laborious steering my ship," Ralph says.

I jerk my head, wondering if he's fucking with me. "Where did you hear that?"

Grace smiles slightly.

"I don't know. I think RT Creative may be the top architectural firm in the country," I say.

Grace grunts curiously. "I think that crown goes to Metropolis. Perhaps Carter in red could expound."

Carter opens her mouth and then, after a few beats, closes it. Her eyebrows furrow as if she's been hit by a bright light. "Well, um…"

Grace chuckles. "I didn't mean anything by you being Carter in red. You look great tonight. Doesn't she, Robert?"

"Fantastic," I say without a pause. "But you know, the numbers speak for themselves. Carter may be a brilliant architect, but she doesn't crunch the numbers."

"Right, right…" Tom says, waving me off.

I lift a hand to put him on hold. "Wait. Grace, aren't we still on the same team?"

Her eyes shift from Ralph to Tom.

"Tom," Hannah says, "RT Creative is working with Elise Stein. We spent the entire afternoon making our plans cohesive."

Servers bring the first course.

Grace leans forward to unblock herself from the guy's arm and look at me. "Is she referring to the plans you drew up this afternoon in the house you rented in Alexandria? You're renting for two months? That was quite presumptuous of you."

She's loving every minute of thinking she has me by the balls.

Hannah scoffs, shakes her head, and mumbles, "She's such a bitch."

"What did you say?" Grace snaps.

Hannah pushes her hair out of her face. "Whatever you thought you heard me say, that's what I said."

The two women scowl at each other.

Ralph touches Grace on the arm and shakes his head. "No need to insult our friends."

"She's not my friend," Hannah says.

Carter clears her throat. "Um, excuse me, Tom. Where can I find the bathroom?" Her eyes are watery, and her skin is flushed.

Tom points over his shoulder. "That way and to the left."

Carter gets up, and I keep my gaze on her as she speed walks out of here.

"You're the one who sold me out," Grace says.

Hannah scowls at Grace, shaking her head. "You're so self-absorbed, Grace Kennedy." She sets her cold glare on Tom Roth. "Too bad you're too stupid to see you're siding with the wrong team. She's a lazy-ass, talentless hack."

This dinner has already gone awry, but I'm too concerned about Carter to care.

I leap to my feet. "Excuse me."

Hannah and Grace stop insulting each other as I gust out the dining room and follow Tom's directions to the bathroom. When I get there, the door is closed, so I knock.

"Yes." Carter sounds as if she's crying.

"It's me. Robert."

It takes a moment, but she finally opens up. Her pretty face is close to the narrow slice of space between the edge of the door and the frame.

"What do you want?"

"Would you let me in?"

She assesses me. The space between us expands. I walk into the bathroom and close and lock the door behind me.

Carter runs the sink faucet.

"Have you been crying?"

She snatches a paper towel off the holder and wets it. "Yes."

"Why?"

"Because we're being played, Robert. And I put a shitload of work into the fucking blueprint." She wipes her eyes and then slams the wet napkin into the wastebasket.

My body is sending me mixed messages. I want to grab her, kiss her, and do it in Tom's bathroom. That would be a big *fuck you* to him. And I want to grab her and hold her until she stops crying.

"How could he do this to me?"

"Who?" I ask.

"Stu."

My heart drops. "Stuart Beatty? You call him Stu?"

She studies my expression and then rolls her eyes. "It's not what you think, Robert. I'm not fucking my boss. Been there, done that."

I crack a smile, and so does she.

"He used me—that's all. I just put it all together. This morning he asks me to represent the company at this dinner tonight. All I'll need to do is show up, looking my best." She crosses her arms and shakes her head. "When I walked in and saw Grace and Ralph, I wanted to get the hell out, but then you walked in."

"Ah, I see. Grace wants to make me think she's not working with Stuart Beatty, and that's why you're here, representing Metropolis."

Carter's mouth tightens more as she continues shaking her head. "I just don't know if I can work for someone like that."

I use my thumb to rub her tears away. "Hey…" I gently lift her chin. "Can I kiss you?"

Her lips press together in a slight grimace.

"Please?" The longer I stand this close to her, the harder my dick gets.

She nods stiffly.

Our lips touch, and my throat grows thick as our tongues touch. Her mouth tastes like red wine and mint. The deeper the kiss, the more I want to devour her. I suck the skin at the side of her mouth into my mouth. She tosses her head back and moans. When I lift her feet off the floor, she so easily wraps her legs around my waist. Her dress rips, and I set her down on the top of the counter, spread her legs, and snake my fingers around the crotch of her panties. Carter takes my shoulders, shoves my chest against her mouth, and moans as I slide two fingers into her pussy. I pull back so that I can see her face as I rub my middle and index finger, shifting in and out of her and scraping the top of her vagina. I can hardly stand it as her mouth falls open and she pants.

"I want to hear you, baby," I say.

Carter nods wildly and moans at the top of her lungs.

I can no longer take it. I impatiently fumble my belt buckle loose, unzip my pants, and pull them down. My erection springs forth and clings to my stomach. I'm so hard. All I can think about is being inside of her deliciousness. I pick her up off the counter. My adrenaline makes her featherlight. I pin her against the door, stuff my dick inside her heat, and shift in and out of her. Every plunge into her pussy feels so fucking good. I want to blast inside her.

"Oh, Robert," she sighs and smashes her lips against mine.

Our tongues swirl around each other. Her fingers clench my shirt and pull me closer. Her pelvis is meeting my thrusts, and she's squeezing her already tight pussy tighter.

"Oh, fuck," I groan. My balls clench. My dick jerks. "Oh," I repeat as I let loose inside her.

Someone pounds on the door.

"What the fuck are you doing in there?" It's Tom.

Carter's eyes widen in sudden panic.

"Talking!" I say.

"The fuck you are. How about you get the fuck out of my fucking bathroom!"

I can't stop grinning and loving that I'm getting under his skin. The fucking douche. "We'll be out shortly."

"Now!" he shouts like a helpless child.

"I'm so canned," Carter whispers.

I put my lips next to her ear and whisper, "Believe me, I have AMLP sewn up."

She blinks as though she's hearing something she just can't believe. "You do?"

"I'm going to go back to the table, but you have ten seconds from the time I sit down to get the hell out of my house," Tom says.

I kiss Carter's lips. "I do, baby."

She pulls down the hem of her dress. "Then explain."

"I will. As soon as we get the fuck out of here."

CHAPTER ELEVEN

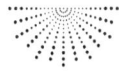

ROBERT TANGO

I've pulled up my pants and zipped up, and Carter has cleaned herself too. We're getting ready to walk out of the bathroom.

She puts her hand on the knob and then quickly turns to me. "You swear you have AMLP?"

I kiss the side of her face. "Jack Lord and I are partnering for East Coast projects. Before AMLP went to Tom Roth, they begged Lord Construction and Development to take it."

"And he's taking it now?"

"Yes, and I'm his architectural partner."

"Does Tom know this?"

"He will tomorrow."

Finally, she chuckles. "And we just fucked in his bathroom."

"He fucking deserves it. He's a tool."

"You mean the tool box."

We laugh, and I get to taste her mouth one more time before she opens the door and strolls into the dining room with the confidence I want her to have. However, I see that Hannah's gone.

Grace is shaking her head. "Classy, Carter."

"Being that you're the queen of the classless, I won't take that as a compliment." Carter snatches her purse off the back of her chair.

"And, um, since you've got the contract with Tom over there all sewn up, I'll just leave as well," I say.

"Tell your girlfriend that she might as well fly back to San Francisco and fuck you some more. She's fired," Grace says.

Carter's already out of the dining room. I stop just before I make it out and turn around.

"You're doing the hiring and firing for Beatty now?"

Grace crosses her arms and smirks. "I'm running the San Francisco office of Metropolis, and my dad is chief architect."

"Then that means you quit."

She winks. "You made it possible."

Grace is referring to the clause that lets her quit

if she wants. I figure it's best for her to move fast on dissolving the contract before she finds out she's just bought a lot of swampland.

"Well, you better move fast, daddy's girl, because tonight, I'll be talking to my lawyers, and I will make it impossible for you to work for me and him at the same time."

Grace narrows her eyes.

Tom wiggles his fingers at me. "Bye now," he says dismissively.

I could punch him in the throat, but it's too late —I've already delivered a blow. I stroll out of the dining room like the lion he wishes he could be.

CARTER IS IN THE CAR AHEAD OF MINE. SHE HAS THE same compact vehicle she used to drive in San Francisco. I'm certain that her transportation of choice is still her motorcycle. It was a beauty, and she took excellent care of it. Shit, we just fucked in Tom Roth's bathroom. I let my desire get ahead of me. She deserves more than that from a man, from *me*. I wonder what she's thinking now. Does she feel embarrassed? Ashamed? Dirty? I wonder…

CARTER REMINGTON

To fuck in a bathroom during a business dinner—that wasn't Carter's style at all. She looked through the rearview mirror. Robert was driving right behind her. When it came to him, she was ultraconfused. He was so hot for her sexually, and vice versa. Could that be it? Could they be all chemical reaction and no solid relationship?

She groaned and rubbed her eyes. Maybe she should ask him to go home tonight. At dinner, Robert had told Tom she was a brilliant architect. He at least respected her work. But he might not tolerate her shit.

"I have a lot of shit," she whispered. And she sure as hell wasn't going to hide it so that he could accept her and "love" her.

She pulled in front of the house. Fortunately, her roadside assigned parking space wasn't taken. Nine times out of ten, someone would steal it and stay until the morning. Once, she'd stood by the offending car and waited for the person to return, and it turned out to be an elderly couple. All she could think was, *shit*, and she smiled at them, went back inside, and crawled into bed to make up for the sleep she lost while trying to catch an offender.

Robert automatically knew to drive up and down and around the block until he found a parking spot. Carter turned off her car, got out, and stood in front of her building, waiting for him. She could feel Mrs. Morris's eyes on her from above. She wanted to look up and confirm it, but she didn't want to let the woman think she condoned the spying. At times it felt creepy.

Finally, Robert came strolling up the sidewalk. His long strides and confident posture reminded her of a handsome avenging angel. All of a sudden, the sexual energy she'd felt in Tom Roth's bathroom rushed through her. She gave in to the urge and looked up as though Mrs. Morris had the answer to the question Carter was asking herself at that moment. However, there was no one standing in the woman's window, and on top of that, her lights were off.

Carter grimaced. She was sure Mrs. Morris had been up there, watching her diligently. Perhaps it was in her head. Maybe it was always in her head, and if she'd just let herself look, she would've discovered that a long time ago.

Robert was near enough that his entire handsome face glowed under the spray of streetlight. He was grinning, and so was she.

"And this is where you live?" he asked, standing so close she could feel his life radiate all over her.

The tips of Carter's fingers tingled, and so did her toes. "Yeah," she said, looking away bashfully.

"It's nice."

"Tomorrow I'll be unemployed and unable to pay my mortgage."

Robert cupped his hand under her chin and gazed at her in a way that said *Don't be ridiculous*.

Carter dipped her head toward the door. "Come on inside, and I'll..." The idea of having sex with him again quickened her and frightened her.

Robert placed his arm around her waist, and together, they walked up the stairs. Her hands trembled as she unlocked the main door. There was nothing she could do to get them to stop. Robert gently massaged her shoulder, and that helped a little. Once inside, they took the staircase that separated her place from Mrs. Morris's. They were almost to the top when the first lock on Mrs. Morris's door clicked.

Every muscle in Carter's body tightened as she

tried to outrun her neighbor's progress. *Not tonight.* Not while Robert was with her.

Just as they climbed the final step, Mrs. Morris's door opened, and Carter was forced to stop and acknowledge her. However, her neighbor looked different than usual. She wasn't wearing a scarf around her winter-white hair, and she had on a long, thick white gown.

"Robert," Mrs. Morris said.

Carter nearly choked in awe. How did she know Robert's name?

Robert grimaced as if he was trying to place her face. "Yes, ma'am."

Carter stood very close to him, figuring soon she'd have to halt her neighbor's kookiness.

"Lizzie isn't well," she said.

He jerked back. "Lizzie?"

Carter studied Mrs. Morris, who looked disheveled, almost as if she were sleepwalking. "Mrs. Morris, do you need help getting back to bed?" Carter had helped her back into bed three times before. The first time, she'd been up late and happened to glance out the window after working six hours straight and saw Mrs. Morris pacing up and down the sidewalk. She ran out and brought her in before anyone could come by and take advantage of her. The other two times—once very early in the morning and once late at night—the elderly woman had been sitting on the step, gazing off into nowhere.

Mrs. Morris smiled, and Carter was relieved to see the expression that let her know her neighbor was all right, at least in the moment. "I'm fine, darling." Her smiled dropped as she took a quick glance to her right. "Lizzie wouldn't let me sleep until I told Robert she wasn't well."

Carter turned her curious glare on Robert. He was as pale as a ghost. She quickly whipped her face forward. Mrs. Morris was already closing the door. Carter and Robert stood there as the first, second, and third bolt locked.

"I'm sorry about that," Carter said.

"How did she know my name?"

She shrugged as she shuffled through her sense of reason to find an answer. "She might've heard me talking about you with one of my friends."

After a moment of staring, perplexed, at her door, Robert smoothed out his eyebrows and nodded tightly.

"I'll just…" Carter opened the door to her townhome.

Once inside, Robert sat down robotically on the

sofa. She wanted to offer him a drink of water or something, but instead, she quietly sat down beside him.

"Is she a psychic or something?"

Carter shook her head emphatically. "No way. She's just an old woman who lost her husband. She gets lonely sometimes." Her memory quickly went off course from the things she told herself to make Mrs. Morris sound saner.

"Well…" She sighed. "She does talk to her dead husband. A lot. Like he lives there with her or something."

Robert slowly turned and faced Carter. "Do you want me to tell you who Lizzie is?"

Carter gulped as her mouth went dry. All she could do was nod.

"Elizabeth Riley, who was once Elizabeth Tango."

Carter frowned. There were a few options. She could have been his sister or his…

"She's my mother."

CHAPTER TWELVE

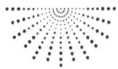

ROBERT TANGO

*C*arter hands me the glass of water. Vodka would've been more appropriate over a year ago, but these days, all it takes to settle my nerves is an ice-cold glass of agua. My blood is racing through me because of what that woman said. How the fuck did she know my mother's name? Was she saying that Elizabeth Riley's ghost was standing next to her, and if so, does that mean my mother is dead?

I bury my face in my hands. "Fuck," I mumble under my breath.

"You want to talk about it?" I look up. Carter has changed into a pair of pajama bottoms and an oversized T-shirt, the sort of outfit a woman wears when sex isn't on the menu.

I hesitate. "I don't know."

"Well, when was the last time you saw your mother?"

I sigh forcefully and then pause to notice how her legs are squeezed tightly together and her arms crossed firmly. "I don't know—ten, fifteen years, maybe longer than that."

"Jeez, that's a long time."

"She's not the kind of mother you visit."

Carter's eyes expand. She looks scared. I'm afraid that if I unleash my shit on her, she'll run for the hills.

"Go on," she says encouragingly.

My eyes go up, and then I sigh with relief. "You sure you want to hear this?"

"I want to hear everything about you."

A knot in my heart twists, and it takes all my willpower not to draw her against me and hold her for my fucking life.

Then I tell her all about my mother neglecting me after my dad died and how even today she won't admit what she did. Carter already knows a lot of this because I spent most of the years after my father died living with Vince's family.

I've now kicked my shoes off, and I'm slouching on her sofa.

"I never told anyone this, but her first husband after my father died showed up in my room one night and crawled in bed with me."

Carter gasps. "He didn't…"

I gulp. "No," I say, feeling the relief. "Because I slid out of bed before he could grab hold of me, ran to my closet, got my twenty-two, and aimed it at his balls."

Carter closes her eyes and shakes her head. "Shit, Robert. No kid should have to do that."

"It's reality, baby. The next morning, he told me this strange story about the grizzly killing the female bear cubs. Later that day, I was telling Vince all about his grizzly comment, and Ann heard."

"And that's why you lived with Aunt Ann?"

I gaze off without focus. "I was glad that was all she had to hear. The other part was just too shameful, you know?"

Carter rubs my back consolingly. I hadn't realized I was resting my elbows on my thighs. I think about sitting back, but her hand feels like the kind of consoling I've been waiting my whole life for.

"That's one of many things I love about Aunt Ann. She's so brave when it comes to stuff like that. Most people would look away—out of sight, out of mind—but not her," Carter says.

I beam at Carter, having no idea what to say next.

"So do you wonder?" she asks.

"Wonder if my mom is alive or dead?"

Carter raises a finger pointedly. "Mrs. Morris didn't say she was dead. She said that you should see her."

"Maybe see her in the grave? I don't know."

We fall silent, and I sit back. Our shoulders are touching, and her being this close feels natural.

Carter yawns.

"Should I go?"

"No," she says quickly. "I mean, you don't have to."

I chuckle. "You put your blousy pajamas on, which generally signifies no sex."

"Do we have to have sex to sleep together?"

I rest my head on the sofa and turn to look her directly in the eyes. "Absolutely not. I'm just glad to be here with you."

She yawns again.

"Are you ready to go to bed?" I ask.

"Yeah, I guess," she says.

I stand up, and so does she.

"Where's your bed?"

She points to the staircase. "Up that way."

I hold her hand, walking her in that direction.

"So, Robert?" Carter says as we slowly take one step at a time.

"Yes," I say warmly.

"If Stuart fires me, can I come back to RT Creative?"

I guide her against me, holding her tight. "Baby, my doors are always open to you."

Carter's mouth opens and then closes. How delicious her lips look, so kissable, but I want to respect her wishes. If I kiss her, then it will be hard for me to get my fucking libido under control. She makes me want to experience her in every way possible.

She gulps. "Thanks," she says, out of breath.

I smirk. "You're welcome." I let go of her and take her hand. "Now, let's finish getting you to bed."

We make it to her room, which is designed nicely. A teardrop glass chandelier hangs a few feet away from the foot of her king-sized sleigh bed, the sort of brand you buy from a luxury hotel's catalog. She has nice, sleek furniture pieces made of fine wood. The light is warm, and I can see the egg-shaped bathtub from where I stand.

"I like how you designed it up here." I sit on one side of the bed.

"Thanks," she says and crawls under the covers.

I take off my pants, socks, and shirt and follow her lead. Once I'm under the sheet, I gather her into my arms. "Don't worry about your job, baby."

She looks up at me. Her eyes are so vulnerable. "I love that you're calling me baby."

I smile. "It feels natural. I want to give whatever this is between you and me a try."

She smiles, kisses me on the cheek, and then whispers, "Kiss me."

My body stiffens. "What if I can't stop?"

"Then take me."

Our mouths meet, and I kiss her. The fire in my loins stirs, but I also want to put her at ease. I'm in this for more than sex, and I'm glad she is too. Finally, our mouths part. I kiss her deeply on the forehead and cheek and then gather her body against me, holding her closely. "Get some sleep."

"Okay," she whispers.

I kiss the top of her head. She kisses my forearm. And together like this, we fall asleep.

CARTER'S ALARM BUZZES. I KEPT HER CLOSE TO ME all night long, and damn, did it feel good. She stretches forward to stop the noise, and I'm forced to let go of her but only for a few seconds. After the chiming stops, Carter snuggles against me, and I wrap my arms around her again.

"How did you sleep?" she asks.

"Good. Real good."

"I wish the day had never come," she says with a sigh.

"We're still on for tonight, aren't we?"

She squirms in my embrace, and I lessen my hold so that she can turn to face me. "Yes." She kisses my lips, and my boner grows firmer. Her hand wraps around my erection and shifts up and down. I close my eyes and suck air. There's no doubt she's telling me what she wants, and I want it too.

I guide her onto her back, use my knee to open her legs, and slip into her warm wetness. "Shit…" I gasp as the blood swirls in my dick.

I'm overexcited. Carter's gasps and moans seem a thousand miles away. It's satisfying to know I'm pleasing her, but I'm even more gratified myself. Slow and steady. I shift left, right, sliding against her walls. Um, this feels so damn good. In and out, in and out… my balls clench. My dick jerks.

"Ah!" I squeeze her tight until my orgasm passes.

I lie, completely content. Damn. I wish I could keep it going, but we both have to get on with our day.

"How was it for you?" I ask, hoping it was as good for her as it was for me.

"Fantastic." She squeezes me and kisses me on the cheek.

I close my eyes and relish the way her lips feel on my scruff. I'll take that sensation with me throughout the rest of my day.

CHAPTER THIRTEEN

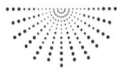

ROBERT TANGO

*I*nstead of leaving DC during rush hour, I walk to a corner café that's down the street from Carter's place. I order a Denver omelet and a hot cup of coffee, find a quiet corner, and check emails on my phone.

My plan worked. I spooked Grace last night when I warned her to move fast because I'm going to stop her from leaving my company. I have an email from Richard. Grace's lawyer submitted her resignation this morning. I call him, and we discuss making sure we legally remove her from the position, effective immediately. He also received the contract from Lord Development and Construction. We spend an hour going over the particulars. Basically, in certain regions, we are architectural partners with them. He also updates me that at this very moment, Tom Roth should be finding out that the Atlantic Metropolitan Library Project is finalizing the contract with Lord Development and Construction, which means Metropolis is out of the running. I'm satisfied as hell after hearing that, which makes breakfast go down easy.

I'm about to get up to pay my bill when I look over to see Carter's neighbor sitting at the table next to mine.

I jump, startled. I didn't see her walk in. "Good morning, Mrs...."

"Ethel," she says with a twinkle in her eyes.

Her smile is contagious. "Then good morning, Ethel."

"Have you called your mother?"

Suddenly, last night rushes back to me in full force. I remember how Ethel gazed off as though someone or something was standing next to her.

I clear my throat. "Um, no, ma'am."

Ethel stares beyond the window. "It sure is a nice day. I was born and raised in Idaho. My husband brought us here in 1964. He was a civil rights lawyer. I never met a man with a heart like his until I met you. Oh, that lovely girl. She's a lucky one. You love her, don't you?"

I don't know how to answer that. Also, there's something pretty amazing and frightening about what's going on right now.

She stands up. "I'll answer that for you. You love her," she says as if she knows my heart better than I do.

Out of respect, I spring up out of my seat to stand with her. I smile tentatively because I'm still kind of messed up by last night's encounter.

"So, um, Ethel, this Lizzie…" I can hardly believe I'm going to ask this. "Did she say she was my mother?"

"Why, yes, dear."

Deep down inside, I quicken with fear. "And she saw me?"

"Yes, dear."

My mouth is dry, and I'm struggling with how to ask the next question.

"She's not dead. Not yet," Ethel says as though she can read my mind. She takes my hand in hers and pats the top of it. "You will go see her because you're a good man. Lizzie has something to tell you."

I'm choked up, wondering what my mom could have to say to me. Another part of me is yelling, *Fuck Elizabeth Riley.*

Ethel pats me on the chest. "You'll do what's right."

She gives me one last smile before walking out the door. I stand for a moment, recounting my wins. I won the account. I got rid of Grace. I'm starting a new relationship—a real one, different than any other I've ever been in. My life is fucking amazing. So why the hell can't I get my mother's face out of my head? And why in the hell do I feel like shit?

CARTER REMINGTON

Carter was twenty-seven minutes late for work that morning. She was never late. After spending the night with Robert Tango, something in her had changed. From day one of working for Metropolis, she'd been full of anxiety. The firm was three times more competitive than RT Creative—heck, four times.

As she walked through the cubicles, head up, she felt relaxed even though people were pretending to not see her. The air was filled with turmoil. Word probably had already spread about her interlude with Robert Tango, which was proven when her friend Camille slyly gave her the thumbs-up.

Carter winked at her, owning her success in love and, fingers crossed, also her career. Of course, Stuart did not disappoint. As soon as she got to her desk, she saw two things: her computer was gone, and there was a note on top of the desk from Stuart that said, "Please come see me NOW."

She stood in front of her desk. It looked so barren without the computer, the one thing that she'd had her nose stuck in since the day she arrived. She wondered what could Stuart want other than to shame her about screwing Robert in the bathroom at Tom Roth's house. He would use it as an excuse to fire her, and it was a good one. But what had he been thinking, sending her there as a smoke screen? He had taken her off the account that day! What a tool.

Robert had asked her to trust him, and although it was difficult for her to trust anyone but herself, she decided to give it a try. Regarding Stuart Beatty, she could choose to walk out and leave and not give him the satisfaction, but what would be the fun in that?

Carter turned her back on the small cubicle. She would never return to that space again. Eyes followed her to Stuart's office. He was on the phone, rubbing the back of his neck. When he saw her, he cut his eyes away from her and swiveled his chair to face the window.

Boy, was he pissed. She considered alleviating his burden by just turning around and leaving. Seeing how stressed he was took away a lot of her anger.

"Carter's here." He paused. "Yes. I got it." He hung up and whirled back around. "Sit down."

Carter hesitated. She had two choices: sit down and entertain him, or leave. It was time to truly think about what she wanted because whatever she decided next, there would be no turning back.

She folded her arms. "I'll stand. Where's my computer?"

Stuart tipped his head to the side. "I insist—sit."

"And I also insist."

He laughed bitterly and then resettled in his seat. "The technical unit has your computer."

"And what for?"

"You know what for."

"So you're firing me?"

"The stunt you pulled at Tom's is grounds for firing."

The anger in Carter welled up. "I mean, are

you really going to sit there and pretend that you didn't send me to Tom Roth's house without a purpose?"

"Yes, I sent you there for the purpose of representing our firm, and you did that by fucking the enemy in the bathroom." He said that loud enough for everyone to hear.

Carter realized he was trying to shame her. Truth be told, it was unprofessional to fuck Robert in the great Tom Roth's bathroom. She'd known better, but she hadn't been thinking clearly at all. Robert made the first move, and she responded. Since she was already pissed about Stuart toying with her, she wanted to show what she thought about it by fucking in the bathroom of the guy whose ass Stuart had been kissing from day one of her employment. Carter realized she was definitely unemployable in the industry after pulling that stunt. Hot gossip like that traveled fast. Not only that, but Robert also could've sullied his reputation. So she had to think fast—faster than she ever had before.

"Who said we were fucking?"

He grunted in shock. "Are you denying it?"

"Did he see us?"

"He heard you."

Carter raised a finger pointedly. "But did he see us?"

Stuart narrowed his eyes to slits. Carter knew she had him in checkmate.

"I may have been angry and voicing that in the bathroom because I figured out that you had taken me off AMLP and then sent me to Tom's house just to throw Robert Tango off your scent." She made sure to say that loud enough so that everyone could hear.

"What? That's ridiculous."

She refolded her arms. "Really? Because I saw you, Stuart."

"You saw me where?"

"At Bagels & Café with Ralph Kennedy, which means you had been talking to Grace, and she's been feeding you lines about Robert and me for some time."

Stuart's mouth fell open. Just then, his computer beeped, and he looked at the monitor. Something had captured his attention. He grabbed his mouth and clicked. Carter watched his jaw move and blood drain from his face as he read. Her stomach turned somersaults. Had Robert come through?

Stuart narrowed his eyes to slits. "Do you know anything about this?"

It was time to put a look of surprise on her face and play stupid. "About what?"

Stuart studied her with that same look on his face. "Forget it."

"Okay," she sang, unaffected. "Anyway, as I was saying, so you could imagine how angry we were to find out that not only had you betrayed me but Grace deceived him. What Tom heard was not sex but us expressing our anger."

Stuart's computer beeped again and again, and then his phone started ringing.

"We're going to have to pick this up later."

"But you just fired me."

He grimaced. "I didn't say anything about firing you."

"Then I quit."

He picked up the phone and smashed his hand over the receiver. "You're not quitting." He removed his hand. "This is Stuart," he said bitterly.

Carter sniffed disdainfully and turned her back on Stuart. She thought there was no better time than the present to make an exit—a real exit.

CHAPTER FOURTEEN

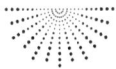

ROBERT TANGO

*I*t's late morning by the time I make it back to Alexandria. I sit in the driveway, staring blankly at the front door. Unfortunately, I can't shove that conversation with Ethel deep inside and deal with my mother only when I'm ready because I'll never be ready. Elizabeth and I wrote each other off a long time ago. I need to know why the fuck a clairvoyant woman is sending me messages on her behalf from some great beyond that's not exactly the afterlife.

I want to pound the steering wheel because Elizabeth has found a way to disrupt what was supposed to be a triumphant day. I can't just not call her, can I? Carter's neighbor is a nice woman, but she could be a loon. Maybe she did hear Carter say my name out loud. Maybe she lucked out with the name Lizzie. She didn't say Elizabeth, my mother's legal name. But... everyone calls her Lizzie.

I grit my teeth and shout, "Fuck!"

I hop out of the car, slamming the door behind me, and trot to the house. The front door's unlocked, so I walk right in. Hannah's voice is coming from the study. She sounds excited and not in a good way. I stop to take a few deep breaths before I go in there. It's probably no surprise where I spent the night. Tonight will be no different. I want Carter to sleep in my arms again. Hell, I want to call her right now and make sure she's fine. Stuart is probably giving her hell, and the thought of her enduring his nonsense aggravates me to no end.

I'm first inclined to run up to my room, shower, and change out of my suit. But I can smell Carter all over me, and right now, that's the scent I want to keep absorbing. So I get control of myself, man up, and face the music.

"What a bitch," Hannah says.

When I make it through the doorway, she's slumped in a chair, shaking her head. At first I think she's referring to Carter, but then I see her black eye.

"What happened?" I ask.

"That fucking Elise Stein is what happened."

Sarah widens her eyes as though the world has just come to an end. "They got into a fight last night."

Hannah thrusts herself forward. "After the scheme she pulled, she had the nerve to show up at an event I invited her to."

Sarah widens her eyes and sighs gravely. "It was so…" She wiggles her head.

She need not say more. I can only imagine.

Hannah looks like a pouting child. Normally she's fashionably put together, but this morning she wears a wife-beater with no bra and a pair of loose, overwashed jeans with holes in the knees. Her hair is wrapped in a knot on top of her head, and she looks as if she hasn't slept a wink.

"She hit me first," Hannah says.

"She pushed you—she didn't hit you," Sarah says.

Hannah throws her hands up. "What's the difference?"

Sarah grunts impatiently. "You could've just walked away, Han. It was horrible. The two of them"—she shakes her hand at the ground—"all over the floor, brawling like UFC fighters."

I work my hardest to try to picture the two women clawing and punching each other. "I take it you weren't throwing kiddy punches since you have a black eye."

"I should sue her," Hannah grouses.

"You can't because you started it," Sarah says.

"Whose side are you on anyway?" Hannah snaps.

"Yours, but you were wrong. You should've just ignored her."

"Not when she came over here yesterday and pretended to be working as partners with us. What she did was betrayal of the worst kind." Hannah flops back in the armchair. "We lost, Robert, so…"

"Who lost? We didn't lose."

Hannah narrows her good eye. "What do you mean?"

I sit behind the big desk in the office and start from the beginning until I reach the part where I'm partnered with Jack's company on AMLP and other projects moving forward.

Hannah and Sarah can't contain their grins.

Hannah grabs the sides of her head. "Oh my God, really?"

I raise my right hand. "That's the whole truth and nothing but the truth."

She smashes her finger against her chest. "So I'm the interior designer?"

"I want you to assemble a team, but yes, as we've already agreed, you'll run RT Creative Interiors."

Hannah and Sarah grin at each other. It's apparent they've been working with each other for a long time.

"Then that means we're moving to San Francisco," Sarah sings and twists jubilantly in her seat.

I smile and look at Hannah. "Has the team arrived?"

"They're in the day room. The furniture was taken out yesterday, and ten desks were delivered this morning," Sarah says.

"While you were out with your girlfriend," Hannah says, fluttering her eyebrows jokingly.

I bob my head thoughtfully. Maybe I should just come out and say it. "She is my girlfriend." She isn't really—not yet—but it's certainly what I want. I avoid looking at Hannah.

She tilts her head curiously. "Then you're totally off the market?"

"Yes," I say with my shoulders pulled back confidently.

"Totally?" Sarah asks.

"Completely."

Hannah pushes herself to her feet. "Great, then it's official. I like it when a man comes out and says he's no longer available. Believe me, I'm one for respecting that."

I tip my head to one side and then the other, studying her. Hell, I believe her. "Thanks, Hannah."

"You're welcome. Now, I have better ideas than the ones Elise had." She spirals her hands in front of her as though she's visualizing those ideas and then pats me on the back. "I think we should capture a certain ambiance. I'll show you what I'm talking about."

Hannah makes it to the doorway.

"But what about this?" I say, pointing to my eye.

She throws up her hands. "Who cares? We won. I feel like new!"

I toss my head back and laugh.

THE TEAM CLAPS WHEN THEY HEAR WE'VE SECURED

the project. I introduce Hannah, and just as I thought, Matt, Justin, David, and Brent stare at her as though she's finger-licking delicious.

"Wait. What happened to your eye?" Matt asks.

Hannah picks up a marker off the stand. "I didn't duck."

That's all she has to say before she goes right into her interior-design plan. The way she stands at the white board, marking up nearly every inch of it and talking the details without subtly using her sexuality to keep their attention, tells me she's the real deal. Grace has a way of running her fingers through her hair, twisting her neck a certain way, or subtly posing to keep the guys from losing interest. She wears a lot of makeup too. Hannah is without makeup, and this is not the first time I've seen her that way. She's confident about what she does and has superior interpersonal skills. It's pretty much luck that I landed her on my team in this capacity.

I leave the project in my team's hands and head upstairs to change into something more comfortable. As soon as I make it to my room, I call Carter to ask how her morning went. She gives me a play-by-play on what happened after she showed up for work.

I'm grinning as I slip on a fresh T-shirt. "You told him we weren't having sex in the bathroom."

"That's the story, so let's stick to it."

I chuckle. "That's some quick thinking on your part, and I like it."

She gives a long sigh.

"Then you're ready to join my team?"

Carter goes silent. I expected more enthusiasm than that.

"If you'd rather not, then…"

"It's not that. I put so much work into the Metropolis proposal, and to see it go up in flames the way that it did…"

I drop my suit pants. "But you can work with us. Share your ideas."

"That's easy for you to say. You're the boss. The minute I join those guys, they're going to feel as if I'm a one-woman show because of you."

"That's not true, babe."

"Robert…" She sighs. "It's very true, especially with Matt, Justin, and Brent. I'm pretty sure they're on this team."

"Yes, but…"

"I choose you, Robert," she says quickly.

Those words tug on my heart, and I sit on the

side of the bed, allowing my brain to repeat them over and over again.

"I want to work for RT Creative again, but in San Francisco with you."

"When are you coming back to San Francisco?"

"Immediately," she says.

"Then you'll stay with me in Russian Hill."

"That would be nice."

Damn it—I'm smiling my ass off. Nothing about the plans we've made scares me. "Okay then. But we're still on for tonight?"

She giggles. "We're so on, dude."

I laugh. "You want to come hang out at the house?"

"Does it have a pool?"

"Yes, it does."

"Then give me the address!" she says.

I tell her the front door will be open and give her directions on how to find the study, which is where I'll be. I also ask her to bring a change of clothes for tonight's date.

When I make it back to the study, I go right to work even though I'm eagerly awaiting Carter's arrival. Sarah stops by my desk to show me twelve different office buildings and spaces near the construction site, some in DC proper and a few outside the city. I tell her that I want to see them all in three days' time, and she sets up viewing appointments with the realtors. Now that I've finalized the contract with Lord Construction and Development, I get my own development team on the phone and challenge them to use our new associates as leverage for ten new projects that we never would've gotten first consideration for without our new partners. I work with Personnel, getting out announcements for staffing the East Atlantic office. I confer with Richard and Gabe about the agreements I just made with Jack.

Hannah and I have just finished going over her qualifications for new personnel.

"Great." She sits back confidently in her chair.

That's when Carter appears in the doorway. Her eyes shift between Hannah and me before landing on my face. "I'm here," she barely says.

She's standing there in dark jeans and a T-shirt with her motorcycle jacket thrown over one shoulder and a helmet in her hand. "Hey, babe."

"Well, hello, Carter," Hannah says.

Carter smiles, clamps her helmet under her arms, and walks into the office to shake Hannah's hand. "Hi, and congratulations on your new gig."

Hannah shakes her hand. "Nice duds. Are you in a riding club?"

Carter looks down at herself. "Oh, no, I just like riding my bike, and I have to wear the right clothes to protect myself from the elements." She tilts her head and frowns. "What happened to your eye?"

Hannah snorts. "I got into a fight with Elise last night."

"Like a fistfight?"

Hannah points to her face. "Hence, the eye."

Carter jerks her head. "I don't think I've ever gotten into one of those before."

"Me neither! That's probably why I lost."

Carter and I laugh.

I've been so taken by Carter's presence that I forgot to rise to my feet. I stand and give her a hug and quick kiss. "Glad you finally made it."

"I had to do some things first."

"So you're here to join the project?" Hannah asks.

"Not this one. I'm here to swim."

Hannah sits up. "Oh?"

"Yeah. I figured after all I've been through, I should take a break."

Hannah grunts thoughtfully. "You know, I might

join you. The chlorine and salt are good for healing."

Carter's eyes dart to my face and then back to Hannah's. It's clear she's still a little leery about Hannah's intentions regarding me. I figure it's time she discovers what they really are.

"That's not a bad idea," I say. "After the Smithsonian-museum brawl, you should take the rest of the day off to relax, unwind, and work on that black eye Elise gave you." I wink to let her know I'm joking.

Hannah hops to her feet. "You don't have to convince me. I'm all for that."

I kiss Carter, and she and Hannah walk out of the office together. Hannah's going to show her to my room. I am slightly nervous Carter isn't buying Hannah's friendliness, but I'm sure by the end of the swim, she'll trust Hannah more than she does now.

My cell phone rings, and I trot back to the desk to answer it. I look at the name on the screen. It's Zoe.

"Yep!" I say, feeling pretty content with the world at the moment.

"Um, Robert." She sounds sad.

My mind goes to the worst-case scenario, which

means the deal fell apart, and she was the first one informed about it. "Yeah, what is it?" I take a deep breath and try to get a grip. Richard wouldn't share the news of a contract break with her before he tells me.

"I just checked your messages. And I'm really sorry, but I've been backed up for a few days. I mean, really sorry."

"It's okay," I say impatiently. I want her to hurry up and get to it.

"A doctor from Twenty-Nine Palms Regional Hospital called. Um, your mother is in a coma, and they don't think she'll last the week. He wants you to call him."

"Twenty-Nine Palms?"

"It's in California."

I touch my temple while closing my eyes. That fucking Mack truck is back, and it's running me over a hundred times. What is she doing in California anyway?

"Robert?" Zoe says with caution.

I clear my throat. "Email me the complete message. I have to go. Talk later." I've never hung up on anyone before saying good-bye, so I wait.

"Okay…"

"Good. Talk later." I hang up.

My head feels numb. I shift in my seat, unable to find comfort. What in the hell am I supposed to do? I thought Elizabeth and I were clear. She stays away from me, and I pretend she doesn't exist. Why in the hell is her doctor calling me? I thought she would've had more kids to fuck up and over by now. I pick up the stapler and shake it. I want to lob it at the wall, but this isn't my house, nor is it a mature way to handle my issues. What would Dr. Mahoney say? I play the conversation in my head.

"Doctor, I fucking hate my mother."

"Hate is a strong word," Dr. Mahoney would say. "If you had five minutes to say something to her, what would you say?"

I would go as blank as I'm going right now.

"Okay, then. Could you live with the fact that she may die and you will never have the opportunity to see her again?"

I would shrug. "Maybe."

"You and I have been doing this for a while. We know that you're angry with her. Have you ever told her why?"

I would try not to roll my eyes. "Of course not. The last time I saw her I was fifteen, almost sixteen."

"Does your inner child have anything to say to her?"

The doctor has asked me this before. I bawled on her couch. That was my answer to her question.

"Okay. Let's try this. Can the man that you are now help the little boy inside say what he feels?"

I stare at the portrait on the wall. It's a ship-wreck with millions of diamonds and jewels spilling out of it, suspended in midair. I focus on one diamond in particular. Seconds tick by as I listen to what the hurt kid inside me feels. Abandoned. Angry. Worthless. Afraid. Helpless. He feels as though he never mattered to her, so why should she matter to him?

"But didn't she come visit you recently?" Dr. Mahoney would ask.

I frown. My eyes burn. Fuck, I will not fucking cry. I tighten my mouth and fight those fucking tears.

She did visit me. And Ethel, Carter's neighbor, was the perfect conduit.

I clear my throat and say out loud, "Yes, she did."

There's a soft knock on the frame of the door. I can barely make out who's standing in the doorway, but I blink my attention back to the moment and look.

I flinch, taken aback. "Elise?"

She's holding a bouquet of purple-and-white flowers. "Can we talk, please?"

Her lower lip is swollen, and she has a bruise on one cheek. It seems Hannah did get some good punches on her. I should be angry as hell at Elise, but then it hits me: I'm the man who gives people the benefit of the doubt. That's why I hired Grace in the first place. That's why I hired Matt after he tried to blackmail me. Hell, why shouldn't I go see Elizabeth for the last time and give her the benefit of the doubt too?

I hold out my hand, gesturing for her to sit.

She shakes her head. "No. I just wanted to stop by and give you these."

"Flowers?"

"Purple-and-white hyacinth to say I'm so sorry." Her eyebrows gather. "Really, when we sat down and revised our plans, I had every intention of working with you. I was excited."

I nod. "Okay, then what happened?"

Her shoulders droop as she sighs. "I got a call from Tom, and he said he was going with

Metropolis, and I had no choice—I had to be in since I signed a contract with him."

I readjust in my seat. "Oh."

"I tried to tell Hannah last night but…" She shakes her head. "She just kept yelling at me, telling me to leave. I told her I had just as much right to be there as she did. We started pushing each other, and before we knew it, things got out of control. We're in the fucking gossip rags this morning." She exhales as she looks off. "I stopped smoking three years ago, but hell, I need a cigarette."

I twist my mouth as I think. Hannah and I came to Washington and made some bad mistakes. I fucked in Tom Roth's bathroom, and she brawled in one of the world's most famous museums. Thanks to Carter's fast thinking, my sin may have been washed away. But next, we have to figure out how to run holy water over Hannah's iniquity.

"Are you still interested in working with us?" I ask.

She scratches her scalp. "I don't know… I don't think Hannah would…"

"Let me worry about Hannah. Are you interested or not?"

Elise sighs deeply. "I'm interested."

I sit back in my seat and steeple my hands in

front of me. "Good. We'll give Hannah time to cool down, and then I'll be in touch."

"Okay then…" Elise looks at the flowers in her hands and then walks over to sit them on my desk. She tilts her head to study the bouquet. "They aren't beautiful. You would think 'I'm sorry' flowers would be more radiant. Instead they are arduous and expensive. Kind of like my mother."

I narrow my eyes, scrutinizing the purple-and-white petals. "Right… Right."

CHAPTER FIFTEEN

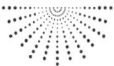

CARTER REMINGTON

*C*arter patted herself on the back for not hyperventilating when she saw Robert and Hannah sitting in his office as if they were old college buddies or something. All she remembered was that Hannah had wanted him enough to make some major moves on him at the wedding. And now she was running his interior-design conglomerate, which seemed sort of fishy. She didn't know what sort of game Hannah was playing, but on the bright side, Robert seemed to trust her in business matters, so that counted for something.

Carter looked at herself in the oblong floor mirror. The piece added a nice touch to the room's contemporary décor of white lacquer, black leather, and silver metal. She brought a black bikini, and heck, she looked pretty skinny in it. Apparently, she'd missed a couple of meals she shouldn't have missed while working hard on the AMLP. The more she thought about how Stuart had sucked so much time and energy out of her life, the angrier she became.

Carter slipped on her white see-through cover-up—which only came down about three inches past her butt—took her cell phone out of her jacket pocket to bring with her, and walked to the swimming pool. She wanted to go kiss Robert one more time but thought better of it. He was working. Plus, the backyard was in the opposite direction.

Like most, she could walk through the hallway and check messages on her phone seamlessly. Rico had texted her five times and asked her what happened. His last text read, "What about Grace?"

Infused with anger, she typed, "What about her?"

"Hey, Carter?"

She jumped to face the opposite direction as her heart raced.

Matt, her ex-boyfriend, touched his chest. "Sorry to startle you."

Carter took a deep, settling breath. "That's okay."

He grimaced. "What are you doing here?"

She held her hands out. "What does it look like?"

His eyes roamed her form, and then he gulped. "So… Metropolis lost the account. We have it now."

"I know."

They fell awkwardly silent. Carter could hardly believe they used to be a couple. Matt wasn't a bad guy, but he was no Robert Tango. Robert was a real man—direct, confident, no innuendo. He just went for what he wanted. Also, Robert was refreshing in that he knew people weren't perfect so he never held anyone, including her, to some unattainable standard. She could be flawed and not have to worry about Robert judging her. She couldn't say the same for Matt.

Finally, she got tired of standing there silently and lifted her hand. "Okay, good luck on the project." She was almost able to turn completely around and walk away.

"So how do you like it here in Washington?"

Carter sighed hard. "You want to know exactly why I'm here and what my connection is with Robert, don't you?"

His eyes expanded as he shook his head. "No…

I mean, sure. If there's something going on between the two of you."

"Yes. We're seeing each other."

Matt's entire body stiffened. "Wow. Long distance?"

Carter figured he might as well hear it now. "Not for long."

He rubbed the back of his neck. "I'm not asking because I'm still into you. I'm over you."

"Good. Now, good luck." She turned her back on him.

"But if you're back, then…"

Carter faced him again. Matt was scratching his temple as if it pained him not to say what he felt. However, Carter already knew what ailed him, and for the first time ever, she felt as though it wasn't her responsibility to put him at ease. So she left him standing there, tormented, and walked out to the pool.

Her cell phone chimed before she reached the lounging area. Rico had texted, "I'm still interested in her."

She was fuming. Her thumbs banged on the screen as she tapped out, "Then ask Stuart. Leave me alone about her." After the message finished sending, she turned off her phone.

Hannah was sitting on a lounge chair, sunning, in a white, sexy one-piece. The weather was nice— hot and muggy but way better than the cold Carter had experienced before summer arrived. She was a little confused about what to do next and whether she should sit beside Hannah and ask her to be straight with her. Was she still after Robert, and was she a snake in the grass, waiting for her opportunity to strike?

"Carter," Hannah called as soon as she saw her.

Carter didn't hesitate as she walked over to Hannah, whose eyes roamed up and down her figure.

"Nice body," Hannah said.

"Likewise." Carter sat in the lounge chair beside her.

Hannah flipped on her side to face her. "So we didn't get off on the right foot because I was all about being a bitch. But I didn't know Tango too well then."

"Okay?" Carter said, not quite sure what was coming.

"I just heard he was hot and liked to fuck, and now he was rich and successful too."

Carter's frown deepened. None of what

Hannah said showed that she wasn't trying to lure away the man Carter was falling for.

Hannah closed her eyes and sighed deeply. "Damn, none of that came out right. What I'll say is this. I can never be into a man who's not into me. And Tango, he's a rare breed—one of those guys who's pretty singular."

"Singular?"

Hannah nodded. "Yeah. A singular guy is one who can fuck all of creation when he's single, but once his heart lands on a sole object, that's all his dick wants."

Carter couldn't help but chuckle. She remembered how Hannah and Monroe had bickered like sisters at the wedding, and the truth was the two of them were more alike than not.

Carter made the OK sign with her fingers. "Got it."

"Good. Now,"—she popped to her feet—"let's swim!"

"Yes, let's." Carter stood.

Hannah grinned. "You want to run and dive and then swim laps?"

Carter feigned a serious look. "Sounds like the best way to approach it."

Hannah laughed and then straightened up to

mirror Carter's expression. "Then you dive left, I'll dive right, and I'll meet you at the other end."

Carter laughed and led the charge. Hannah followed as they darted toward the crystal-clear swimming pool and dived into the lukewarm water.

CHAPTER SIXTEEN

ROBERT TANGO

"Wow," Carter says and sits down on the side of the bed. I just hit her with some hard news. "If you're going, then I can go with you?"

I tell her about how I spoke to Ethel, her neighbor, in the café this morning and later received a call from Zoe about my mother.

I sit beside her. The concern in her eyes makes my heart hammer. I massage her neck softly. The more I feel the softness and heat from her body, the harder I get. Carter curves her neck. I take it as her way of asking for more. I guide her down onto the bed. She squeezes my swollen cock, and the sensations make me close my eyes and suck air.

"Yes. Come with me," I whisper.

"I will, and I will." She sighs.

INSTEAD OF PAINTING THE TOWN RED TONIGHT, WE take a rain check, and I drive Carter home so she can pack a bag. I forgo telling Hannah about the conversation I had with Elise earlier. I've stirred up enough shit in my life to know that people are more apt to forgive and forget two weeks after the confrontation.

Carter and I expect Ethel to come out and greet us when she hears us walking up the stairs, but she doesn't. I'm pretty relieved about it because I'm still not sure I'm going to go through with the trip even if I booked the red-eye out from DC to Dallas/Fort Worth, where we'll take a charter flight to Palm Springs International Airport. The more I think about seeing Elizabeth, awake or in a coma, the more I'd rather continue avoiding her.

I sit against the headboard of Carter's bed and wait for her to pack for our trip. I'm shocked by the size of the suitcase she just swung on top of the bed. I took her for a light traveler.

"I use a lot of products," she says when she sees the look on my face.

It's enough to make me chuckle. Carter struts over from the other side of her room to stand in front of me. She rubs the side of my face. "I love it when you laugh."

I could take her right then and draw her between the sheets and forget about the world and all of our problems. But that wouldn't be a practical way of dealing with my shit. It's time to be an adult and face my hard truths.

I pet her on the ass, which has become one of my favorite parts of her to touch. "I'm willing to laugh some more for your benefit."

Carter lowers her face until our mouths meet, and we kiss. It starts slow. Before long, she's on my lap, and I'm stroking her modest-sized breasts and squeezing her hard nipples.

"Again?" I say.

"Again."

I unsnap her pants, unzip them, drop her sweet ass onto the bed, then take her pant legs by the hem and pull them off. The sight of her plump pussy makes my mouth water. The scent of her moisture releases into the air. We don't have much time, so I can't dine on her the way I want. Instead, I stomp out of my pants. She spreads her legs, and the sight of her creamy lips makes me stab her with an erection so firm I'm ready to come right away. But I don't. I close my eyes to feel all of her warm wetness, enjoying the stimulation of her pussy. We kiss the whole time. Tasting her mouth is almost as good as being inside her. When I come, the feeling is so good I white out for a few seconds.

"Shit," I say as I lie on top of her body.

"Umm..." She moans and shakes with the residuals from our lovemaking. "Fuck."

Afterward, Carter and I shower together. She washes my back and front, and I wash hers. When we're clean, we dress, she finishes packing, I take her suitcase, and we leave. As soon as we walk out, Ethel's door opens. Now that I'm high on the pleasure chemicals swirling around my brain, I'm ready to tell her that I'm on my way to visit my sick mother. However, a woman who looks to be in her fifties steps out of Ethel's apartment.

The woman glances at me, and then her curious eyes settle on Carter. "Are you Carter?"

Carter clears her throat. "Um, yes."

The woman's sullen expression turns into a slight smile. I can clearly see the pain in her eyes as she and Carter shake hands.

"My name is Linda Morris. I'm Ethel's daughter. My mother died this afternoon."

Carter turns her stunned expression on me and then back on Linda. "But… how?" Carter says, clinging tightly to my waist.

"She was fine this morning. I ran into her in the café." I point toward it. "The one on the corner."

Linda chuckles softly. "Smith's. She goes there every morning."

Linda tells us that every Tuesday at eleven she comes over to play bridge with her mother for two hours. Today when she came over, Ethel didn't answer. She tried her key but couldn't get in because the bolts were locked. That was when she knew something was wrong. She called a locksmith, who called the fire department, and they broke the locks.

"Mom was sitting on the sofa in her favorite flowered dress." Linda looks off. "She went peace-fully." She smiles tightly and sighs. "Mom always said that's how she wanted to go." She faces Carter again. "Our paths never crossed, but she liked you a lot. She said as long as you were around, I didn't have to worry."

Carter grimaces as though she's still trying absorb what we just learned. "I liked her too."

Linda raises a finger. "I see you have your suit-case, which means you're going somewhere, but could you wait here for a second? Last night she called me and said she wanted you to have something."

Carter glances at me. "Last night?"

Linda pulls down the sides of her mouth and shakes her head. "I should've known then." Her voice cracks. "I'll be back."

Linda goes into the apartment. Carter wraps both her arms around me, pressing her cheek on my chest. "I can't believe this."

"Me neither." I kiss her on the forehead. Now, for sure, there will be no turning back. I have to acknowledge the request of the sweet lady who said I was a good man, one of the best she'd ever met.

CARTER HOLDS A BLUE PORCELAIN PENDANT ON A silver chain in front of her face. "Why do you think she gave me this?"

We're in the car on our way back to Arlington before heading to the airport to catch our flight, which gets off the ground in four hours. The gift came with instructions. Carter is to take Linda's address so that one day she can mail her back the silver chain. "Ethel said you would know when that was," Linda had told her.

"I can't guess, but I'm starting to trust that she had some sort of second sight."

"Like a sixth sense, right?"

"Something like that."

Carter sighs and puts the pendant and chain back into the box. "I always suspected it but didn't want to believe it. The real world is taxing enough."

I glance at her with a smile. She smiles back, and once she puts the blue silk box into her purse, I take her hand, and we interlace our fingers. We don't let go until I park in the driveway, and we kiss.

Carter waits while I go inside and put together a quick bag. I have far fewer products than she does, so it only takes me twenty minutes. I wonder why she opted to stay in the car. I imagine it has something to do with facing the team members as my girlfriend. I like the sound of that. Carter's my girlfriend. I should've asked her inside because no one's here. They all probably went out to dinner—knowing Hannah, that's exactly what happened. I don't think she knows how to be in before midnight, which is another reason we never would have worked as a couple.

When I make it back to the car, Carter is asleep.

Last night was full of us touching one another and being acutely aware of the other's presence. I was too excited to get any good sleep. I'm sure she was too. Plus, she swam all afternoon with Hannah, and then later, the rest of the team joined them. I stayed back in my office since I had to get work out of the way in order to free up time to make this trip. If I could have conked out, I would have.

We make it to the airport, which, as expected, is crowded even at this time of night. I park as close as I can to the terminal and carry my bag—and roll Carter's suitcase—into the airport. After checking our luggage and getting through security, we make it to the gate, where she sleeps some more on my chest. Seeing how tired she is after the hassle of airport screenings and what feels like miles of walking to our gate, I wish I'd chartered the entire flight. From this point on, if Carter is with me, I'll do just that. I want her to be comfortable. She's precious to me. I can see myself falling in love with her, sooner rather than later.

We soon board. At least we're sitting in first class. I ask Carter to stay awake long enough to eat something.

"Gosh…" She yawns with her head resting on my chest. "I didn't know I was so tired."

I kiss the top of her head. "We had a long day."

"Robert?" she says in a low voice.

"Yes."

"Is this real?" She lifts her head to look me in the eyes. "I'm really with you like this?"

I gently kiss her lips. "Yes, you are. And I'm the one who has to keep pinching myself because you're more than I ever deserved."

She smiles. "I beg to differ."

I crack a smirk. "No, I do."

She chuckles softly. "So funeral next Tuesday and then what?"

"We head back to San Francisco."

"Together?" she asks.

"Are you ready?"

She nods, and I drink in the way her face brushes against my chest.

"So am I," I say.

The flight attendants serve salty teriyaki chicken for dinner. No matter which airline, the food is never superb, which is another reason to fly charter. Finally, it dawns on me. Who am I trying to play modest for? I can afford my own aircraft. I'd better buy one—especially now that I have a woman I need to get back home to, and not when the commercial-airline flight schedule says but when I say.

I rest easy, knowing that I'm okay with making life that much easier for myself. We make it to Dallas and are chauffeured to our airplane and take off in less than thirty minutes from when we arrived. Carter and I take our respective seats, lay them out flat like a bed, cover ourselves with blankets, and sleep until our flight lands in the tepid early morning in Palm Springs.

CHAPTER SEVENTEEN

ROBERT TANGO

*T*here's nothing like the desert. The city of LA was once a wide-open desert beside the Pacific Ocean. That was one reason I used to stay there months at a time—to enjoy the dry heat sprinkled with a tiny bit of moisture from the ocean. But Palm Springs, well, it has its own special kind of magic. It's four in the morning and already seventy-two degrees. A car has driven us to the gate, and Carter and I walk through the open-air terminal slightly more rested and ready to make our way to my house west of Palm Canyon Drive North, on the same side as the tramway. I live in one of the oldest and classiest neighborhoods in the city.

A car waits out front to take us to our destination. We get in, and Carter and I agree that we want to ride with the windows down.

"It's kind of warm out there," the driver says.

"We know," Carter replies.

He shakes his head but rolls all four windows down anyway.

"How often do you come to Palm Springs?" Carter is still resting on my chest, which I think is her favorite place to lay her head.

"When I'm in LA for a prolonged period of time, I will stay out here for a few weekends out of the month."

"And your mom lives in Twenty-Nine Palms, which isn't that far. You never knew she was so close?"

"I never knew she left Colorado."

"Wow." Carter lifts her head to gaze out the window. We're driving up Roman Road. She's focusing on the structures up the path and the homes and businesses with drought-proof landscaping.

"I used to come here a lot because Palm Springs is an architect's dream world," I say.

"Oh, I agree."

The car turns right down Indian Canyon, and we're in the heart of classic Palm Springs. Every building tells tales of the 1950s when people smoked cigars, wiggled their brows, and snapped their fingers to music by the Rat Pack. It's not only that, but the energy that flows through the streets and sidewalks can heal a wounded heart if you let it. For a moment, I forget that we need to be at the hospital in five hours, which means we still need to get in my silver classic Benz, parked in my garage, and drive east up to the high desert. Instead, I close my eyes, take a deep breath, and relish in the here and now.

THERE'S BUZZING.

"Oh…" Carter moans and scoots out of my grasp.

I set the alarm clock before we lay down to catch a little more shut-eye. I would reach over and slam it off, but Carter is between it and me. I'm used to sleeping in this bed alone. I've never brought a woman back to this place. It's her first time, and now she has the job of scrambling to hit the alarm.

"There," she says and flops back down on her back. "This is the most comfortable bed I've ever slept in. Wait…" She raises a finger. "The second most comfortable bed I ever slept in. Your bed in Napa—oh my God, that was like sleeping on a cloud."

I reach out and draw her back into my body. "Same brand and model."

"Really?"

"Yes." I gently kiss the back of her neck. "I can have the same bed delivered to my house in Russian Hill although the one that's there is pretty remarkable."

She flips around to face me. "I'll take your word for it."

We smile at each other for a few beats.

Her smile fades slightly. "Are you ready?"

I hold my breath and then let it out slowly. "As ready as I'll ever be."

"Then we'd better get going, right?"

"Yes, we'd better."

Carter runs her hand gently across my bottom lip. "You are so handsome, Robert Tango."

I frown a little. That's a big jump from *Are you ready?* "Thank you."

"If you'd rather do this alone, then I'm okay with that."

My frown deepens. "Why would you say that?"

She shrugs. "Because…." She closes her eyes.

Carter doesn't have to say it—I can see the reason written all over her face. She still can't trust that I could want to be with her and only her.

"Listen, baby. I want you and no one else but you. There's a lot about me that you've yet to discover—hell, that I've yet to discover. I want you to see those parts and not run away from them. And I'll see every part of you and stay right here by your side. That's the kind of relationship I want with you. This is real, baby. As real as it gets."

Carter's smile forms slowly and culminates with an enthusiastic nod. "I want that too," she whispers thickly.

Tears stream from her eyes, and I kiss them away.

ON THE WAY OUT, I GIVE CARTER A QUICK WALK-through of the rest of my quintessentially Palm Springs midcentury modern house.

"When I bought the compound, I had it completely gutted and renovated from the inside out."

"It's impressive," she says.

We make it to the garage, and I pull her against me. "And so are you." I kiss her, and yet again, my head is weightless. Is it just me, or does she feel the same way too?

CARTER REMINGTON

Carter's head spun as Robert's strong mouth and tasty tongue meshed with hers. Their lips parted, and he walked her to the passenger side of the vintage Mercedes Benz and opened the door for her.

"Thanks," she said. Robert never failed to open the car door for her. No guy she'd ever been with had done it more than twice, and that was usually before they had sex a second time.

The inside of Robert's car looked and smelled like brand-new leather. The seats were white and lined with gray tubing. It was a sexy old car for a sexy young man.

Soon they were well on the way to their destination. Robert remained quiet for the most part. He would only glance over with a smile and ask if she was okay. She said, "Fine," and five minutes later, he asked again.

Carter studied his profile. She had been in this situation many times before. After her parents divorced, her mother, who was devastated by the split, used to put on the same sort of smile and ask her over and over again how she was doing. Carter had watched her mother when she thought no one was looking and noticed the way she sat in the recliner, gazing out the window with a trembling chin. Her eyes blinked rapidly whenever Carter tried to have a conversation about school or something pertaining to the house. Then one day her mom drove her to a soccer match in Culver City because Carter had missed the team bus. She was sixteen then. Her mother narrowly avoided a collision on the 110 freeway and then, while transferring to the 10 freeway, stopped abruptly to avoid banging into a two-ton truck. Carter's mother had zero reaction to either incident. A realization had hit Carter like floodlights in the face. This despondent woman was who her mother had always been.

When the car inched its way across the bridge to the 405 freeway, Carter's mom smiled at her and asked, "Are you okay?"

Carter reached out and rubbed her mom's

shoulder. "Mom, I'm fine, but maybe you should make sure you're okay."

And then *slam*. Her mom rammed the car in front of them.

On the day Carter graduated from college, her mother gave her a graduation card with a key and a note that was worth more than anything she could've ever given her. Her mom wrote about that day of the car accident in the card and thanked Carter for changing her life. It was then that Carter knew she, herself, mattered. In a postscript, she wrote, "I know you want a motorcycle, but your dad and I agreed this is a better option." They'd bought her the fuel-efficient hybrid car that she still drove as an alternative to her motorcycle.

As Robert drove his car, wearing a similarly strained expression to the one her mother once wore, Carter petted him on the arm. "Are you okay?"

He made a quick move in his seat and then stiffened. "I don't know, you know?"

Carter angled her body to face him. "What are you feeling precisely?"

Robert narrowed his eyes at the mountain path ahead. He had been driving pretty fast up the winding road, and he finally slowed down.

"Squeezed," he said.

"Squeezed?"

"Elizabeth's spirit is forcing me to do something I really don't want to do."

Carter shrugged halfheartedly. "Then turn around and head back to Palm Springs. You're the one in control of Robert Tango. No one can make you do anything you don't want to do, and frankly, you don't owe your mother a thing."

Robert glanced at Carter with a grimace. He rubbed a hand over his face. "You're right. I mean, I know that, but…" He shook his head.

Carter nodded consolingly. He didn't have to say more. She knew. He needed to see the source of his pain, anger, rejection, and everything that having an unavailable mother made him feel. Carter knew about that because she'd needed to experience the same kind of come-to-Jesus moment with her own father, who'd left her mother not for another woman but merely to be free of the life they'd made with each other. Her father still hadn't remarried, nor did he date. She even asked him once if he was gay, and he laughed and said, "No. I'm a man who wants to be alone because that's what I want."

"Then you're a rare breed, Dad," she'd said.

He'd shrugged. "I guess I am."

Robert reached over and gently squeezed Carter's thigh. "Thank you, babe."

She put her hand on top of his. "You'll be okay."

He sighed. "I know."

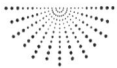

CHAPTER EIGHTEEN

ROBERT TANGO

inally, we pull into the parking lot of the small hospital, which is in the middle of nowhere. Even though I'm shaking like a leaf, I let Carter hold my hand. She squeezes it tighter, and that makes me feel a little better.

Once we're inside, I'm struck by the putrid scent of hospital. It smells like disinfectant, body fluids, drugs, and sickness. I never want to end up in a place like this, lying in a hospital bed. Knock on wood.

We stop at the reception desk. I clear my throat. "Elizabeth Riley."

The woman behind the desk types the name on the keyboard. She frowns. "You said, Elizabeth Riley?"

Shit. I feel my body heat rising. "Yes."

The woman grunts and then types again. "No. There's no one by that name."

I would take that as a sign to get the hell out, but instead, I say, "Someone from this hospital called me and said my mother is here."

"Oh," she says, sounding more hopeful. "What's your name?"

"Robert Tango."

Her eyebrows pull downward. "Oh… right." She fumbles in a drawer and hands us two visitor badges. "She's in room 2303, on the second floor." She can barely look me in the eyes when she says, "It's the intensive care unit."

"What happened? Why is she here?"

The receptionist smiles sympathetically. "The doctor will talk to you. I'll let him know you're on the way."

There's a dick somewhere inside me who wants to stand here and complain until she clues me in more about what's going on with Elizabeth. By her reaction, it's clear she knows more.

But Carter rubs my back, and I give in to the tenderness of her touch.

I nod briskly. "Thanks."

The whole way to room 2303, I want to turn

tail and run. By the time we make it there, the fact that my mom is in a coma hits me. A guy in a white coat is standing next to my mom. She's lying in a hospital bed, out cold, with a tube coming out of her mouth. I presume he's the doctor, and as soon as he gets wind of my presence, he turns to face me.

"Robert Tango?"

"Yes, that's me." My heart has solidified, and now it's weighing me down as I walk closer to the bed, my eyes pinned on the patient.

The woman lying there doesn't even look like the mother I remember. Her hair is salt-and-pepper, she doesn't have a bit of makeup on, and her skin tells the tale of a woman who has had a lot of worry in her life.

"Your mother suffered a major cerebral aneurysm." He goes on to say that they were able to clip the artery and stop the bleeding, but Elizabeth went into cardiac arrest during the procedure. "Currently, she has very little brain activity, and the respirator is breathing for her."

I blink hard a few times. What in the hell am I hearing? And why do I care all of a sudden?

"Wait? Who found her? How did she get to the hospital?"

He gives me the same sympathetic look the

receptionist gave me. "Mr. Tango, your mother *came in off the street*, complaining of a persistent headache."

My hand shoots up. "What do you mean by 'came in off the street'?"

"We believe she was homeless."

I open my mouth to speak, but I feel as if my tongue just swelled at the back of my throat.

"According to the report, the receptionist repeatedly told your mother she had to take her grocery basket outside before she'd be able to see a doctor, but she kept grabbing her head and complaining of the pain."

I snort bitterly. I'm positive they treated her terribly—a homeless woman with no insurance. She was probably at the bottom of their list of priorities. That's probably why he's sticking to the report. He's covering his ass.

My body goes tense. "And then what happened, Doctor?" I say coldly.

"Your mother fainted in the lobby. She was lucky that she was here, Mr. Tango."

I fold my arms. "And she was alone?"

"Yes, sir."

"Then how did you find me?"

"We had no information on her, so one of the

nurses went through her basket and found this." He opens the folder in his hand and gives me a magazine.

It's *MM* magazine, and I'm on the cover. Scribbled inelegantly beside my picture are the words, "My only son. Robert, I'm sorry."

Tears race to my eyes, and I lower my head to rub them away.

Carter puts her arm around me. "Doctor, could you give us a minute?"

"That's okay." I raise my face and clear my throat. "What's her prognosis?"

"We're going to keep her stabilized and hope that she can recover. We have limited resources at this facility. I recommend transferring her to Sacred Heart in Redlands."

Carter and I look at each other gravely. Seeing my mother lying in the bed leaves me only one choice.

"Then let's get it done. Immediately."

The doctor nods briskly and tilts his head. "Just so that you know, this is a very expensive undertaking."

I bare my teeth and look him straight in the eyes. "I didn't think it wasn't, which is why we're doing it, right? Because I'm here to pay for it."

The doctor hesitates, but after a moment of watching me glare at him, he breaks eye contact to look through his folder.

"Then I'll get the paperwork started."

Once he's gone, Carter and I walk over to my mother's bedside.

"I'm so sorry, Robert." Carter rubs my back.

I bring her in closer and kiss her on the forehead. "She doesn't look the same. I wonder what happened. How did she end up in this town, pushing a shopping cart?"

The longer I stare at my mother, the more human she looks. I had always known she was weak and self-absorbed, but she was also resourceful and never had a problem finding a guy to take care of her. I always figured Elizabeth would land on her feet.

"Mr. Tango, could you come with me to fill out some paperwork?" a voice says. Carter and I turn to see a woman standing in the doorway.

"Go. I'll stay here," Carter says.

We give each other a quick kiss and hug before I head out to pay an arm and a leg for my mother's medical care.

In the last seven hours, I've consulted with my physician, who called his buddy, a neurological surgeon from LA, Dr. Russo. He was waiting for the transport team when they arrived. Carter and I drove up from the high desert. After tests were completed, the doctors determined that Elizabeth went into cardiac arrest because she had an enlarged heart. Not only that, but her liver is bad because she drinks too much.

Carter and I stay in the hospital overnight. When I insist she let me book a hotel room for her, she refuses. "I want to stay with you and her."

I nod. "Okay."

She smiles. "Okay."

CHAPTER NINETEEN

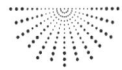

ROBERT TANGO

he last three days have been filled with doctors and procedures. Carter and I did eventually book a hotel room in town. She's there, resting. Last night, I found an old ragged phone book in my mom's things. I went through it and discovered a number for Nora, her older sister. I called her, and she answered.

We've been on the phone for roughly fifteen minutes. My aunt Nora tells me that we've met twice, and I wasn't old enough to remember either time, so I have to take her word for it. She says she hasn't spoken to my mother in seven years.

Something bad happened between them, and she refuses to tell me the circumstances surrounding their falling out.

"Elizabeth is very sick, Robert, and I hope she gets the help she needs."

"I can fly you out here to see her if…"

"No," she says emphatically. "But I can say this for certain. How she treated you broke her heart. She would repeat that over and over again while she was, you know, intoxicated."

I could probably take a stab at guessing what bad shit occurred between them. Nora was the Vince in the situation, and Elizabeth was the Robert. She probably kept taking advantage of Nora's kindness and love until she committed some unforgivable act. And just as Vince forgave me because we're true brothers until the end, I'm sure Aunt Nora is capable of the same.

"Thank you, Nora," I say.

"I'm pretty proud of you, kiddo," she says, changing to a lighter topic. "Hank and I have been following your success for years. You did good."

I sag into my chair and rub my eyes. "Thank you," I barely say.

"Let me know how she's doing."

"I will. Good night."

The next day, Dr. Russo calls me into the office to tell me that my mother has developed pneumonia. Her kidneys are failing, and her heart is swollen again.

He sits back in his chair as if he's overwhelmed by the news he's delivering. "Instead of getting better, she's getting worse."

I nod silently. I'm not surprised. She was in pretty bad condition when she came into the hospital. Elizabeth is in her midfifties, and she looks thirty years older. "Maybe she's done living." But saying that makes me numb inside.

"When this happens, usually that's the case." He shifts in his seat as though he has something uncomfortable to say. "The nurses say you've been here a lot."

I frown, wondering where he's going with this. "Yeah. I have."

"But have you interacted with your mother?"

I sit back and cross my arms. "How can I? She's in a coma."

Dr. Russo smiles tightly. It's clear he's trying to soften me up. Yeah, I haven't gotten that close to her. It's as though I'm paying for it all but watching it happen from a distance.

"If your mother was homeless, then she probably felt alone and isolated. She has a lot of recovery in front of her. By the state of her liver and heart, this recovery includes therapies for depression and substance abuse. It's going to be a long road, Robert. If she thinks she's taking the journey alone, even in her condition, she probably has already given up. Just talk to her. Let her know you're here."

My throat feels as if there's a big rock sitting on top of it. First, I have to admit to myself that I've been thinking that it would be easier if she just went away—better for her, better for me and all the people she's been hurting along the way. But who am I? Not God. Not a judge. I'm her son, but more importantly—and I can say this with the utmost confidence—I'm a decent human being. I feel shit. I can forgive. I can love.

I nod with resolve. "Right. I'll do that."

Dr. Russo winks and steeples his hands in front of him as if he's just scored a victory. "Good."

"Thank you," I say as I stand.

We shake hands, and I head to my mother's room. The whole time, I'm forcing myself to get in the mood for it. What do I say to her? I think about what Dr. Mahoney would say.

"Why did you bring her here in the first place?" she would ask.

"Because I'm a decent man. I couldn't just let her die," I would say.

"But you would be okay if she died?"

I sigh as I enter the elevator with another family. I look up at the ceiling so I won't see the women watching me.

"I wouldn't care," I would say to Dr. Mahoney.

"But she's your mother."

"She gave birth to me, but she wasn't a fucking mother at all."

"Do you have any good memories, Robert?"

"Not fucking one," I would say. But then I'd feel guilty about how angry at her I was, and I'd try harder to find some good memories. "She packed good school lunches for me when my father was alive. She used to wait for me by the door whenever I came home from school. If it was snowing, she would remove my cap and rub my ears to make them warm and then tell me the hot cocoa was on the table." I would frown as this clear memory hit me. "She was the best mother a kid could have when my dad was alive, but after he died, she changed." I would sigh gravely. "I just wanted to fucking fix her, you know? Fix everything."

"You couldn't fix a thing, especially not her. You were a kid."

"I know that."

"Do you?" Dr. Mahoney would ask.

"Yes?"

"Do you think your mom was able to fix herself?"

"What was wrong with her?"

"What do you think was wrong with her?"

The elevator doors open. I make myself smile as I put a hand across the threshold to let the women out first. They say thank you and bat their eyelashes at me. That's another thing Elizabeth gave me—my looks. I step out of the elevator behind the family and walk slowly toward my mom's room.

Carter isn't in there today. She flew back to DC two days ago after Matt sent me an email issuing me his two-weeks' notice. Carter and I both knew he was leaving because of her. I didn't want to let her go back, but only for personal reasons. I would miss having her body against mine as we sleep and then waking up early in the morning and sliding into her warm and wet pussy, making love to her until we ignited. But as a businessman, I had to let her go. Carter would know more about where to set up shop than anyone on my team. And if she knew what to say to make Matt stay, then I wanted her to give it a shot. Was I jealous? Yes. Did I trust her?

Absolutely. So I put her on a charter flight, and she flew straight into Dulles. I'll see her soon, and I can't wait.

So getting back to the question Dr. Mahoney would ask: what do I think was wrong with Elizabeth? She was a newly single mother with no profession and no husband to take care of her or me.

"I think she went to work," I'd say. "That's what the going out was all about: finding herself a new husband and me a new father. But five marriages under her belt, and she couldn't ever get it right."

"Are you angry at her for that?"

I want to shout, *hell yes*. But I understand that I've come too far for that. Shit isn't about me all the time. My mom's problems certainly aren't about me. And she's no perfect goddess, but no one is.

"No. I want to be angry, but in the end, she's only human, and she had her own shit to contend with."

Dr. Mahoney would smile and say, "Then you do forgive her."

I stand by the door to my mother's room and press my fist against my mouth. I want to fucking bawl like a hurt kid. That's exactly what I would do if I were sitting on Dr. Mahoney's couch, having a conversation like the script I just played through in my head. I fucking pull it together, though. I can't go in there all weepy.

Before I go into the room, I put on a face mask and gloves and tie a gown over my clothes. Since she has pneumonia, they're taking special care to make sure no one tracks in germs to worsen her condition. When I walk inside the room, a nurse named Cecilia is changing one of Elizabeth's IV bags.

Cecilia smiles at me. "How are you today, Robert?"

"I'm fine, Cecilia. How are you?"

"Another day, another dollar."

I smile and walk over to stand right next to the bed. This is probably the closest I've ever gotten to my mother. "How is she?"

Cecilia shrugs and then grunts grimly.

"I'll stay here with her for a while."

"That's good," she says pleasantly. "That's very good. And she'll like it if you hold her hand and talk to her—let her know you're here."

"I'll do that."

She's still smiling as she walks out. I guess they're happy that the patient's moneybags son has finally stepped up to do the only thing money can't pay for—give her some real human contact.

I take my mom's hand, and it feels as though bolts of energy shoot through my arm and fill my heart. My head drops, my knees go weak, and I fall down onto the chair that's parked right next to the bed. Every time I try to look at her, my head drops again. Every time I try to speak, the need to cry takes over my throat. So I press my lips tightly together. Fuck, why am I feeling this way? Her hand in my hand is so delicate. I wonder if she was always this delicate. Is this the monster I painted in my head—merely a woman who was dealt a bad hand in life?

Then the first sob comes and the next and the next. I'm bent over her body, weeping as the eleven-year-old kid should have. I have more knowledge now, so I'm not weeping just for me—I'm weeping for her too.

"You're not alone, Mom," I say with tears rolling from my eyes and snot draining from my nose. "I'm sorry I left you alone, but you're not alone anymore."

Suddenly, she squeezes my hand. I blink at her face to clear my vision. Her eyes are slowly opening.

"Nurse!" I shout at the top of my lungs. "Cecilia!"

Cecilia, Patty, and Mary dash into the room. Elizabeth's eyes are still open, and she's moaning, trying to say something even with tubes down her throat.

I step back to let them work.

"Elizabeth, honey, you're doing fine," Cecilia says.

"Go call Dr. Russo," Mary says to Patty, who nods briskly and rushes out past me.

"You're back, honey. Stay with us," Cecilia keeps repeating.

All I can do is watch these women in awe as they do their jobs. I've never been in a hospital this long for any reason, but today, especially at this moment, I have a profound respect for nurses and the importance of what they do.

By the end of the night, Dr. Russo and the team of nurses have Elizabeth stable and comfortable. She's breathing on her own, but they are feeding her oxygen. She's still on the antibiotics, but now that the alcohol is cleaned from her system, her organs are absorbing the medicine and nutrients they're feeding her.

Earlier, I placed a call to Roy Talbot, my

number two. He is handling everything while I'm here at the hospital. The next call I made was to Carter to inform her that my mother was awake and how it happened.

"You were holding her hand?" She sounded shocked and amazed.

"Yeah. I was," I say, sounding just as surprised.

"Wow, babe. She woke up because you were there for her." Damn, I love that sweet tone she used.

I nodded, still teary. "I think so too."

"Do you think it's a spiritual thing? I mean, if you *really* think about what happened with Mrs. Morris, it sure does sound like one."

My heart warmed at the thought. "Perhaps. I'm still not ready to lose faith in the physical world."

Carter chuckled. "Me neither, but I still think it's all connected."

We left it at that for the time being, and I grinned while listening to Carter tell me a story about how she set Hannah up on a date with a guy named Rico who'd initially been interested in Grace.

"Rico may have his superficial side, but he's my friend, and he doesn't deserve someone as evil as Grace."

Finally, the name rings a bell. "He's the guy you dated when you first moved to DC."

"We had one not-so-good date and one very bad date, which led us to conclude that we're better off as friends."

I didn't like hearing about any guy who could've been romantically involved with Carter, but I was happy to hear that Hannah had someone else to be interested in.

We talked some more about missing each other. She hadn't been able to have a conversation with Matt yet because he was avoiding her, but she said she knew exactly where he'd be the next day, so he won't be able to hide then.

Throughout the night, I wake up whenever a nurse comes into the room to change my mom's IV-drip bags, take her blood pressure, draw blood, and the like.

I can hardly keep my eyes open as I watch Cecilia smile at me. "She's going to make it," she says while nodding.

The thought both delights me and frightens me.

CHAPTER TWENTY

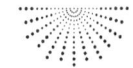

CARTER REMINGTON

THE NEXT DAY

*C*arter got off her motorcycle, took off her helmet, put on her hard hat, and headed toward the construction site. It was impressive to see the Lord Construction tractors, cranes, and forklifts at work. They had already poured the foundation and gotten the framing done. She had never had the opportunity to work with Lord Construction and Development, but everyone knew they were the fastest and most proficient in the business.

She walked down the designated pathway. Construction sites were always the same and never as they were in the movies. Men paid attention to the estrogen that strolled onto the scene but only barely. They were too busy building things. It didn't take long to spot Matt Franks, standing with the site manager. He didn't look happy to see her, and she knew he wouldn't, but she didn't slow her approach.

"I'll see you on the seventh level," Matt said to the site manager and then turned his grimace on Carter. "What are you doing here?"

"I'm here to talk to you?"

Matt's glare roamed the floor. They were being watched. "This way."

Carter followed him out of the structure, down the path she'd just walked, until they had cleared the hard-hat area.

"What do you want?" he asked.

"Is it really either you or me?"

He squinted as if he didn't understand what she was talking about.

"If I'm back, then you go? If you stay, then I can't come back?"

Matt grunted and rolled his eyes. "Did Robert ask you to talk to me?"

"No. I asked him could I give it a shot. He likes your work."

Matt smirked facetiously. "But you're going to always be ahead of me since I can't fuck him."

Carter dropped her head and laughed with an edge. "I figured that was the case. Why are you always competing with me, Matt?" She held her hands in front of her. "Here's the cake. It's a big cake. Here's my piece way over here, and here's yours. Same cake. Big enough for the both of us."

"Okay. What about the fact that I love you, and I can't see you with him."

She rolled her eyes. "You don't love me, Matt. You're fascinated by me. You want to beat me in the race to the top." Carter shook her head emphatically. "But love me? No way. You don't love me."

"But I do."

"You don't, and you know how I know?"

Matt tilted his head, a curious expression on his face.

"Because I've never been myself around you," Carter said. "When I was with you, I couldn't even recognize my own voice. And as long as I was losing, you loved me the most, but as soon as I started winning, you ran off and started fucking Grace."

Matt's Adam's apple bobbed twice.

"Listen—I love Robert Tango, and it's for real. I, like, fart-around-him love him."

Matt lifted one side of his mouth into a crooked grin. "You fart?"

"Yes," she said, shaking her hands excitedly. "All the time. More than my love, Robert is my friend. He doesn't get offended when I know something he's never heard of. Instead of trying to shut me up, he wants to know more."

Matt shrugged. "Well, yeah, that's just the kind of guy he is."

Carter's smile widened and gleamed. "Right! He is that kind of guy and…"

"And what?"

"It's just I don't think my falling in love with Robert should mean he has to lose his best architect."

Matt examined her expression. Carter seized the moment and intensified whatever feelings she thought he saw—true love, hope, and also a tiny bit of masked desperation. The longer he said nothing, the more she wondered if her attempt to convince him to stay on board was working.

Finally, his shoulders slumped, and he sighed. "Okay, then. I'll retract my notice." He cracked a tiny smile. "Plus, I'm into Hannah."

Carter's eyes expanded.

"What is it?" he asked.

Poor guy. He couldn't win for losing. He would more than likely pine for another unavailable woman. Carter was certain that Hannah would see Rico, and Rico would see Hannah, and then sparks would fly.

Carter showed Matt her most convincing smile. "Nothing! I'll let Robert know you're back on board."

"Thank you, but I'll let him know."

She sighed. "Of course you will. Then, I'll see you around—that's whenever you get back to San Francisco."

"You're not staying in DC?"

Carter started walking backward, away from Matt. "Nope. I left my heart in San Francisco." She winked.

He snickered and flung a hand at her. "Oh, get out of here already."

She laughed and jogged back to her bike. The shipping company would be at her house in two hours to send her boxes to San Francisco. Tomorrow would be her last day in her townhome. She'd decided to keep it and rent it to Hannah, who loved the place the moment she walked inside.

Carter couldn't wait to see Robert in Redlands. They planned to drive to San Francisco by the end of the week. Carter knew for sure that once they were together, she would never choose to live so far away from him again—*ever*.

CHAPTER TWENTY-ONE

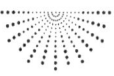

ROBERT TANGO

FOURTEEN AND A HALF MONTHS LATER

"*A*re you ready, babe?" I call, standing at the front door.

Our flight leaves in an hour, but it won't be a hassle since I bought my own aircraft. It's a beauty —even Vince agrees.

"I'm coming!" Carter says from somewhere upstairs.

We've been living together for an entire year. Each day that goes by, I learn more about her and, in the process, love her even more.

"Here I am," she says, running down the stairs, holding the handrail. She used to run down the stairs without holding the handrail, but I asked her to cling to its safety—if not for her sake then for my peace of mind. I wouldn't know what to do with myself if I lost her. I want to live the rest of my life with her by my side.

We embrace after she stops in front of me.

"The luggage is in the car?" she asks.

"All five of your suitcases and one of mine—a very small one at that."

She rolls her eyes sweetly. "I have a lot of..."

"Products. I know."

"Plus, I'm spending the entire day with Maggie, Hannah, and Monroe tomorrow. I have no idea what they have in store for me, but I want to make sure I'm prepared."

I wrinkle my eyebrows. "And that's why you need to take just about everything in the bathroom cabinet?"

She kisses me quickly on the lips. "It's not everything—only half. Plus, Maggie just said bring the good stuff because she wants me looking like a million bucks when we go out tomorrow."

"Humph. Strange."

"Yeah, but don't worry. If you're not there, then I have no one to impress."

I smile. "Now that's what I like to hear."

I kiss her, but we keep it brief because we're pressed for time.

Tonight is my mother's coronation ceremony. She has spent one year in a treatment center in Palm Springs, and tomorrow she's graduating from it. She looked really good the last time Carter and I visited, which was two months ago. The stress lines on her face had smoothed out. She had put on weight and muscle to the point where she looked healthy. She didn't dye her hair, opting to keep the salt-and-pepper because, as she said, it made her look regal. Carter and I golfed with her, and the two most important women in my life clicked over swapping recipes and discussing ways to improve Carter's golf game. Go figure—my girlfriend formed a liking for golf on our very first visit with my mom ten months ago.

After Elizabeth spent her final two weeks in the hospital, she and I had a talk. I gave her two options: let me help her find the best recovery programs, or let me set her up in her own place in a city of her choice and pay her living expenses for as long as she didn't abuse the privilege.

"Which decision keeps you in my life the longest?"

By then I had helped the nurses feed her, bathe

her, and keep her entertained. Elizabeth's complete recovery was a concerted effort, which is why on the day she checked out of the hospital, I bought grand bouquets of flowers for all seven nurses who treated my mother. I wrote personalized messages for each of them, and inside of each card was a check for three thousand dollars—a thousand dollars for each week of Elizabeth's stay.

"Mom," I said, "I will be there for you whichever decision you make."

My mom chose the healthy option. Dr. Mahoney helped find the best recovery program in Southern California, which happened to be in our favorite city, Palm Springs. The program was for people her age, which according to Dr. Mahoney was an important factor.

Carter and I arrive at the compound. The place looks like a five-star resort. We've arrived early enough to find seats in the front row. The ceremony starts, and when Elizabeth sees us, she waves wildly. I think about what Dr. Mahoney said in our last session together. "Robert, pat yourself on the back, and know that you're a good man. And as the saying goes, 'A good man is hard to find.'"

I didn't abandon my mother and stew in my anger and pain—I followed the goodness inside me.

And now look at her; she's even healthier than she was two months ago.

After the ceremony, I take my mother and her favorite friends to dinner. That's when I learn of her plans to stay in Palm Springs. She's moving into a sober living community, and she'll work as a cook in the community cafeteria. Of course, I'll be paying for her house, but I don't mind because she's found her life, and so have I.

CARTER REMINGTON

After dinner with Elizabeth, Betty, Rose, and Opal, Carter and Robert drove back to Los Angeles. Carter was jet-lagged and said she wanted to cancel her day with the girls and stay in Palm Springs to sleep, rest, swim, and relax. But Robert convinced her to trek onwards and stick with the plan, reminding her that she didn't often get to spend the day with two new friends and one new family member, all very busy women who were excited about spending time with her.

Maggie arrived at the house in Pacific Palisades, bright and early at eight in the morning. She rang the doorbell wildly, shouting, "Wake up, Carter!" over and over again.

"She's going to wake the neighbors," Carter said as she rolled out of Robert's arms.

She rushed downstairs to answer the door, and there were Maggie and Monroe, looking cheery and ready for the world. She let them in despite her desire to go back to bed and sleep.

"Get out of the bedroom, Robert!" Maggie yelled as they followed Carter upstairs.

They spent the next thirty minutes picking out her outfits—one for daytime and the other for that evening. They made her say good-bye to Robert.

"Tell him you'll see him, late, late, late tonight," Monroe said.

Carter didn't want to repeat it. They hadn't even left, and she was already missing Robert. She was starting to question why in the world she'd agreed to a girls' day out in the first place. However, Monroe wouldn't let them leave until Carter had repeated the words verbatim.

"I'll see you late, late, late tonight," Carter said though it pained her.

And then they were out.

First, they spent five hours at a spa in Bel Air. After the first body scrub, Carter was happy she'd challenged herself and decided to go. Hannah showed up during their bath time in the warm Roman pool, which they had all to themselves.

"So Carter. When do you think Robert's going to pop the question?" Hannah asked.

Carter stretched out on her back and treaded water. "I don't know. Maybe never. We don't need a piece of paper to know we're in love. Love is written on our hearts."

"Hear that, Mags?" Monroe said.

Carter closed her eyes, but she could hear Maggie push water into Monroe's face.

"So congratulations to Monroe," Maggie said, clapping.

"For what?" Hannah asked.

"She landed her first major acting role."

Carter shifted from floating on her back to standing on her feet. "Wow. Details, please."

Hannah rolled her eyes. Carter and Robert had talked in detail about how jealous Hannah and Monroe were of each other. It was the strangest thing.

"I'm playing a fried news anchor in a new drama," Monroe said.

"It's for Prime D TV."

Hannah jerked her neck and then grunted dismissively. "It's for A&Rt Media?"

"Hey, what's wrong with that?" Maggie said.

"Nothing," Hannah said. "I guess it's always who you know in Hollywood."

"And not what I know?" Monroe roared back.

"Okay, you two. Not now!" Maggie said.

Monroe and Hannah gave each other snide looks and then retreated to their separate corners.

Carter felt trapped in the middle. "Anyway, congratulations, Monroe. I can't wait to see the first episode."

Monroe smiled at her. "Boy, that Tango sure is lucky. You are a good one."

Carter shook her head. It was evident Monroe was flirting with her. She knew Monroe did it intentionally—it was her way of disarming people. It had worked when they first met but not anymore. Now she handled the flirting more in the way Maggie did, which was by pretending it wasn't happening.

After their time in the Roman pool, they dried off and headed to the on-premises salon.

"Remember when I said I could make you more beautiful?" Hannah said.

Carter recalled the night she met Hannah outside Robert's guestroom at Jack and Daisy's place in Denver. The next morning at breakfast, Hannah was insulting her looks. At least that was what Carter initially thought. After knowing Hannah for over a year, Carter realized that she looked for unique beauty in everything and everyone, which was why she was such a brilliant designer and stylist.

"Yes," Carter said.

"Well, this is where you let me work my magic. Are you in?"

Carter looked at herself in the mirror. She had let her hair grow out in the course of a year. Her face was small and heart-shaped, and lately she looked buried in too much hair.

"I'm all yours," she said to Hannah.

The stylist's name was Gianfranco. Carter took solace in knowing that he was the one who maintained Maggie's effortless and sexy haircut. Three hours later, after he'd colored, washed, and cut her hair, Carter looked in the mirror again. She was startled to see a raven-haired beauty looking back at her, an exotic-looking woman with powder-blue eyes.

"Damn, Hannah," Monroe said, leaning over

Carter, who was still sitting in the stylist chair. "I have to give it to you—you've orchestrated a masterpiece here."

Hannah straightened her posture, shocked to receive the compliment from Monroe. "Wow. Thanks, Roe."

Monroe gave her a thumbs-up.

"Glad my new look could broker a peace treaty between the two of you," Carter said.

Hannah and Monroe snickered.

"It was only temporary," Monroe said. "But I love her, so don't worry; we're not going to kill each other."

"Really?" Hannah said, looking shocked.

"Really what?" Monroe said.

"You love me?"

"Of course I do. Love, hate, that's how it's always been."

"But how can we make it different?" Hannah asked.

Monroe narrowed one eye. "Is that what you really want?"

"Yes," Hannah answered quickly.

Monroe walked around the back of Carter's chair to give Hannah a hug. "Then I'm all in."

Maggie clapped. "Yay!" she said, walking in

from the other room. "Now, let's get dressed and go to dinner."

CARTER HAD PUT ON HER NIGHTTIME DRESS, WHICH was a sexy red number that fell over her figure like a sweet kiss. Hannah had applied her makeup so perfectly that all the shading and color seemed to naturally rise from her skin. With her new look and in her sexy dress, Carter would've loved to have Robert be the one accompanying her for the night.

The restaurant was in Hollywood. Monroe insisted that they go through the kitchen to meet the celebrity chef. And so the four women trekked through the alley in their sexy outfits. Monroe knocked on the door, and a kitchen staff person opened it.

"Are you sure we should go in this way?" Carter asked. It all seemed so strange.

"Yep," Monroe said confidently and strolled inside. Hannah and Maggie waited for Carter to enter and went in behind her.

The food smelled divine, and the kitchen staff worked like honeybees and paid no attention to the visitors. Carter was about to ask where the chef was as she moved through swinging doors and into the dark restaurant.

The lights cut on.

"Surprise!" many voices yelled.

Carter stood in front of a big banner that read, "Will you marry me, Carter?" in gold sparkling letters.

Carter smashed her hands over her mouth and looked around the room. Allie, Lexie, Maddie, Anne, Vince, Daisy, Jack, other friends from work, and associates from LA were there.

"Elizabeth." Carter went over to hug the woman who would be her new mother-in-law.

Carter's parents were there as well, and she hugged both of them. Then the crowd split into two halves. Robert walked down a red carpet, stopped in front of her, and kneeled, holding a tiny red velvet box in his hand. She couldn't control the tears. Never in her life had she expected to see a proposal like this.

"I love you, Carter. More than my heart can bear."

Carter wiped her eyes. "I love you too."

He pulled the box open. "Then you'll marry me?"

"Yes!" she said as loud as she could. "Of course, yes!"

Robert sprang to his feet and wrapped his arms around her.

She said, "You got me good."

"It sure is good that I got you," he said, and they kissed until her mind ran in circles.

They ended up having the best night of their lives. The food was fantastic. The friends and family were fun. And they danced until two in the morning, the time everything closes in LA. Then they went home, made love, and lay loose limbed, too excited to sleep.

"Now I know why Ethel gave me the pendant," Carter said.

"Why?" Robert guided her against his naked body and kissed the nape of her neck.

Once she was settled against his nakedness, she said, "It's something old, something borrowed, and something blue."

"She knew I was going to ask you to marry me?"

"She also knew that I would say yes."

Carter turned around to face Robert. "You're a good man, babe."

"And you're a good woman."

Carter smiled from ear to ear. "So… is this our happily ever after?"

"It's our happily in the beginning."

She chuckled. "There's no such thing."

Robert mounted her and sank his blossoming erection inside her warmth. "It's whatever we want it to be, baby."

And they made love until their eyelids felt heavy and their hearts finally settled down and they could fall peacefully to sleep.

THE JOURNEY CONTINUES. READ THE NEXT BOOK IN THE LOVE IN THE USA SERIES NOW!

Say You Love Me (Charlie & Angel) Book 9